HOWARD, LIZ
ISABEL, THE W
(2) 1994 LARGE PRIN F

YO-EIH-559

**PROPERTY OF
ONONDAGA COUNTY PUBLIC LIBRARY**

"Whoever wilfully detains any ... property belonging to any public or incorporated library ... for thirty days after notice in writing to return the same ... shall be punished by a fine not less than one nor more than twenty-five dollars, or by imprisonment in jail not exceeding six months ..."

N Y S Education Law
Section 265

MAY 0 3 1994

**CENTRAL LIBRARY
ONONDAGA COUNTY PUBLIC LIBRARY
SYRACUSE, NY 13202-2494**

SPECIAL MESSAGE TO READERS

This book is published by
THE ULVERSCROFT FOUNDATION
a registered charity in the U.K., No. 264873

The Foundation was established in 1974 to provide funds to help towards research, diagnosis and treatment of eye diseases. Below are a few examples of contributions made by THE ULVERSCROFT FOUNDATION:

A new Children's Assessment Unit at Moorfield's Hospital, London.

•

Twin operating theatres at the Western Ophthalmic Hospital, London.

•

The Frederick Thorpe Ulverscroft Chair of Ophthalmology at the University of Leicester.

•

Eye Laser equipment to various eye hospitals.

If you would like to help further the work of the Foundation by making a donation or leaving a legacy, every contribution, no matter how small, is received with gratitude. Please write for details to:

THE ULVERSCROFT FOUNDATION,
The Green, Bradgate Road, Anstey,
Leicester LE7 7FU. England
Telephone: (0533)364325

Love is
a time of enchantment:
in it all days are fair and all fields
green. Youth is blest by it,
old age made benign:
the eyes of love see
roses blooming in December,
and sunshine through rain. Verily
is the time of true-love
a time of enchantment — and
Oh! how eager is woman
to be bewitched!

ISABEL, THE WOMAN

Isabel had married her chivalrous knight, but only hours after she became a blushing bride, the dream turned into a nightmare. In despair, Isabel rushed back into the arms of her forbidden love. Geoffrey Bernulf was a peasant working on her land, and an archer committed to the King's cause who, despite his skill and loyalty, could be hanged should their indiscretion be discovered. He swore revenge on her husband, determined to make her his own, but then war came to the quiet backwaters of the County of Chester.

*Books by Liz Howard
in the Ulverscroft Large Print Series:*

ISABEL, THE GIRL

LIZ HOWARD

ISABEL, THE WOMAN

Complete and Unabridged

ULVERSCROFT
Leicester

First published in Great Britain

First Large Print Edition
published April 1994

The right of Liz Howard to be identified as the author of this work has been asserted by her in accordance with the Copyright, Designs and Patents Act, 1988

Copyright © 1990 by Liz Howard
All rights reserved

British Library CIP Data

Howard, Liz
    Isabel, the woman.—Large print ed.—
    Ulverscroft large print series: romance
    I. Title
    823.914 [F]

ISBN 0-7089-3059-X

Published by
F. A. Thorpe (Publishing) Ltd.
Anstey, Leicestershire

Set by Words & Graphics Ltd.
Anstey, Leicestershire
Printed and bound in Great Britain by
T. J. Press (Padstow) Ltd., Padstow, Cornwall

This book is printed on acid-free paper

For Brian,
with love.

Fytton Family Tree

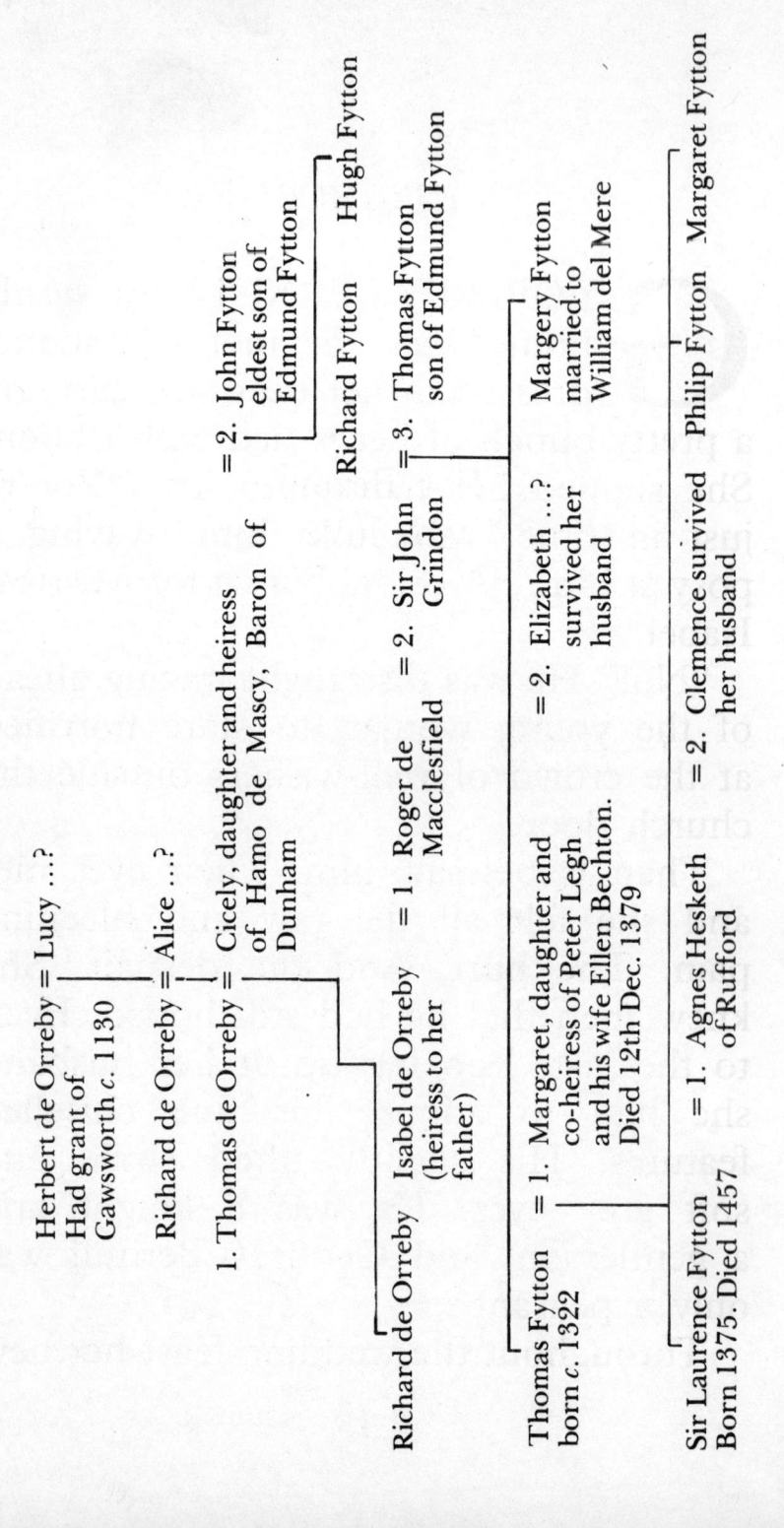

Herbert de Orreby = Lucy …?
Had grant of
Gawsworth *c.* 1130

Richard de Orreby = Alice …?

1. Thomas de Orreby = Cicely, daughter and heiress of Hamo de Mascy, Baron of Dunham
   = 2. John Fytton eldest son of Edmund Fytton
        ├── Richard Fytton
        └── Hugh Fytton
   = 3. Thomas Fytton son of Edmund Fytton
        └── Margery Fytton married to William del Mere

Richard de Orreby

Isabel de Orreby (heiress to her father)
 = 1. Roger de Macclesfield
 = 2. Sir John Grindon

Thomas Fytton born *c.* 1322
 = 1. Margaret, daughter and co-heiress of Peter Legh and his wife Ellen Bechton. Died 12th Dec. 1379
 = 2. Elizabeth …? survived her husband

Sir Laurence Fytton Born 1375. Died 1457
 = 1. Agnes Hesketh of Rufford
 = 2. Clemence survived her husband
   ├── Philip Fytton
   └── Margaret Fytton

Preface

GEOFFREY BERNULF was nearly home when he met Christiana, dressed in her best and carrying a pretty bunch of herbs tied with ribbon. She slipped her hand into his. "You're just in time," she told him, waving a posy at him. "A bridal bunch for Mistress Isabel."

"No!" He was distraught, racing ahead of the young woman to stare horrified at the crowd of well-wishers outside the church door.

Then Isabel saw him. Their eyes met and she felt all the raw and bleeding pain. The hurt. And the despair. She knew then that he had still hoped. Even to the last. Looking up at her husband she had to admire his fine chiselled features. His slightly tilted smile and soft grey eyes. He was a knight and a gentleman, and Geoffrey Bernulf was only a peasant...

Throughout the wedding feast her new

husband smiled that enigmatic smile of his. To his mind words were no longer necessary now that he had gained the cherished manor, tucked conveniently away in the folded hills half-way between London and Scotland. A young boy leaned against John Grindon's chair and he stroked the lad's hair absently. He'd become very fond of Jordon de Bolyn; a clever youth, and one with ambition enough to meet the price . . .

The house was as silent as the grave and Isabel felt herself being lifted onto the bed.

"So beautiful. So pure." Slowly he bent closer, the expression in his eyes all reverence and adoration. The warmth of his face was against the coolness of her exposed flesh, his mouth seeking the proud, expectant nipple. She closed her eyes . . .

Then it was over. Reaching for the torch on the wall he held it high above his head. "I'm sorry . . . " And then he was gone. To his own chamber. Where Jordon waited.

Stumbling from the bed, she reached the window slit. Outside, as first frost glistened, the scene was still and silent, and Geoffrey Bernulf stood, outlined in moonlight, beneath the old oak. "Oh, Geoffrey. Geoffrey," she moaned softly to herself. Salt tears overflowed as he turned away, retracing his footsteps towards the stable, on his way back to Christiana in her tiny cottage, where she would be waiting for him with open arms.

Isabel wriggled into an old day-gown and her bare feet sped over the rush strewn floor of the hall towards the entrance of the tunnel, a short-cut from house to byre. Peasant or not, she loved him. Body and soul . . .

Geoffrey held onto the sobbing woman, wondering if he was dreaming. Only this morning he had seen her married. Only moments ago he had looked up at the window she shared with Sir John Grindon, hating her.

"Please, Geoffrey . . . I cannot tell you . . . Only know that I love you. That I have always loved you . . . If you can forgive me."

This was no act. He held her tight against him, feeling her tremble with every ragged breath. Then taking her in his arms he carried her to the soft piles of hay and lay beside her. Her pale skin was luminous in the half-light; her eyes great pools of sorrow reflecting torment. Tomorrow, she would tell him, but for tonight, he could only help her to forget. Tonight they would explore Paradise together. Because today Isabel, the Girl had become Isabel, the Woman.

1

THIN grey strands filtered through the central hole in the thatch, hanging motionless in clear night air before dispersing to perfume the first frost of winter with wood-smoke. Inside the cottage, Christiana gazed wide-eyed into the dying embers of the fire, her heart beating ominously with every passing second as she tried to read the pictures in the glowing ashes. Where was he? Why hadn't he come to her? With a piece of dry kindling the golden-haired woman stirred the remnants of fire into flame. It had been a day of wildly conflicting emotions.

The morning had been fine and warm, yet with that faint cool tinge to the air which sharpened the senses to the onset of autumn. A mellow sun had taken its time in a cloudless sky to melt soft mists over the near-by river, but by the time Christiana had bound her head with her best white coif and arranged the fine woollen shawl about her shoulders the day had been as bright as anyone could wish for a wedding. Isabel de Orreby, Mistress of Gawsworth Hall since her brother's untimely death, was marrying Sir John Grindon, a close friend, if rumour was to be believed, of none other than King Edward himself! And no one could have been happier about it than Christiana Marton, once known as the witch-girl, but treated with a good deal more respect since the demise of old Mother Marton. It was an event she had long hoped to see. An event which would put an end, once and for all, to Geoffrey Bernulf's ridiculous ideas of owning not only the Hall and all the lands around, but the Mistress too. How many years now had he wasted to that dream? Twelve? Fourteen? Christiana had lost count. All she knew was that once, long ago, she and her sweetheart had plighted their troth on the banks of the River Bolyn and she had given herself to him, body and soul. And if it hadn't been for Mistress Isabel seducing him with promises they'd have been before the rector exchanging rings the week

Peter Bernulf died leaving his son this cottage.

So it was that she had set out this morning with a posy of herbs for health and happiness to give to the bride, with her heart lighter than it had ever been. Geoffrey had marched off in one of his terrible black moods months ago, looking for a fight. Unable to attack Sir John, he had set out to find the King, though whether he had done so Christiana had no way of knowing. The country was in turmoil. Some said civil war! And Piers Gaveston apparently at the bottom of it. Too close a friend of King Edward, it was whispered. Though when she'd mentioned it to Geoffrey, out of curiosity, he'd insisted that the King was as good a man as any of them and seeing him fight side by side with Gaveston against the Scots none could ever doubt it.

Making her way along the path by Three Mile Wood Christiana had been lost to the world as her mind meandered through a thousand little scenes of past events. She'd never been far from these parts, all she'd ever wanted was being here in the County of Chester, and especially this corner. She'd been born here. Her few friends were here. And likely she'd die here. There was no need for her to wander, like Mistress Isabel. Travelling to London. Meeting the King. Pretending she was a woman of fashion and elegance. Well, Isabel de Orreby could pretend all she liked. Those who had always known her knew her true worth. And her darkest secrets! What would Sir John Grindon think of his new wife if he found out the truth? And though Geoffrey might wander off from time to time, following the army in his capacity as an archer, he always returned to the bed he shared with Mother Marton's daughter. No. Christiana had no need to go far. He always returned. Sooner or later.

In the silence of dark isolation a stealthy rustle on the grass-strewn hard-packed floor had the woman turning from the flickering fire-light to peer into the smoky depths beyond.

"Lucifer. Come here, you old familiar. Why aren't you out hunting, eh? There's a moon for it."

The black cat arched its back, straightened its tail and purred loudly as it rubbed its neck against her skirt.

She'd been surprised, but pleasantly so, this morning when the rustling in the wood had turned out to be none other than Geoffrey. Had he been a cat he too would have arched his back and purred. The grin on his face reached from ear to ear and she had squealed with delight as she rushed into his arms. For the moment, the war was over. Gaveston was executed. The King was returned to London. And Lancaster was appeased. Christiana couldn't have cared less about the affairs of State. All she cared about was the fact that he was home. And she hadn't seen him so happy for years! His anger over Isabel's forthcoming nuptials had evaporated. Or so she had deceived herself into thinking.

Moments later he had been running headlong towards the Hall, his eyes wild with anguish. He hadn't known of the wedding. He'd stayed away too long. As Christiana had stood with him outside the tiny church beside the Hall she had watched the naked suffering on his face.

Seen the pain and hurt as the newly-weds emerged. His skin had been white. Deathly. He had stared in an agony of disbelief, rigid with impotence as he saw his plans in ruins. She had heard his indrawn breath. Almost felt the surge of hate flowing through him. Then he had turned to look at her with eyes which didn't see. Slowly and calmly he had taken her in his arms and kissed her as though she was the only woman he had ever wanted. His passion had been controlled, but only enough to reveal its hunger. Yet even as she trembled with the desperate need to be loved by this man, the only one she had ever known, she was fully aware that he was putting on a performance for Mistress Isabel, wanting to remind her of all she was losing by marrying Sir John.

Christiana bit her lip as she remembered his crushing embrace. He was so strong in many ways. And yet so vulnerable. How could he ever have believed that a woman of wealth and standing like Isabel de Orreby would marry a peasant tied to week-work and bid-reaps on her own land? In most respects he had been treated no differently from any of her other villeins. Granted, she'd turned a blind eye to his poaching activities, but that was like to change now that Sir John was lawfully in charge of the estate. He would have to tread a deal more carefully from now on. By marrying a man of the King's Court, Isabel had well and truly put Geoffrey Bernulf in his place. And yet . . . Seconds after he had drawn apart from Christiana the new Mistress Grindon had swooned right away, her husband of a few minutes having to lift her in his arms and carry her into the Hall. Could it be that Isabel . . . ? But no. Christiana stroked the cat's head thoughtfully. It was finally over between them. Isabel had made her choice. Now it was up to Christiana to show Geoffrey that the wife he sought had been living beneath his own roof since the day his mother died.

Lucifer mewed plaintively, moving towards the latched door. "So you too have decided to desert me!" Christiana rose unsteadily from the stool beside the hearth and limped to let him out into the night. The hinge squeaked, mouse-like, in the silence and the black cat disappeared into the shadowed undergrowth, encouraged by the sound into remembering his role in life. Mice. Rats. Voles. They were all one to Lucifer.

Frost sparkled on a blade of grass and the young woman raised her eyes to the pale face of the moon. Where could he have got to? If only she could gaze down on the earth from a midnight sky, seeing all! The truth might hurt, but not knowing was so much worse. Had he left again? Gone off after another fight? To the King's army? To other parts? Other women? Another life? Christiana leaned against the door-frame, shifting the weight from her crippled leg and twisted foot. Over the years her lopsided gait had caused increasing deformity of hip and spine until now, at the age of twenty-seven, the common ache which had plagued her from birth had sharpened itself into needles of pain, piercing flesh and bone alike. Her disability had never caused her heart-ache. Why should it? Geoffrey had bedded her despite it, saying that she had the face of an angel and the body of a temptress. Even tonight, worried as she was, she did not blame Nature's imperfection for her troubles. Her failure came from deep within. She was barren. She had given him no child.

In the distant skies, high over the sleeping town of Macclesfield, quicksilver movement, bright and pure, caught her eye. A star, loosened from its place in the heavens, fell to earth, leaving in its wake a sequined trail across the blackness.

"I wish . . . " Christiana caught her breath. "I wish for a child to raise. I wish us to be a family . . . " She turned to the silent moon. "Goddess of all women, by whose power our course of motherhood is governed, witness my star of fortune. Hear my plea."

* * *

Beside the still-warm stone of the baking-oven Jack Sharpe twisted into another position, scratching at the new line of flea-bites on his left buttock as he did so but not bothering to let go the dream or the slumber surrounding it. His life in the kitchens and stables of Gawsworth Hall suited him very well. Not that he could remember any other life! He'd been fetching and carrying in return for a bite and bed since he had realised that if he wanted to live, he must fend for himself. With eight older brothers, there had been no hope of inheriting land from his father and consequently, no hope of an independent life if he remained at home. By the age of six he had made the corner by the oven his own and by his willingness to run around at Tilda's beck and call had lived well off the crumbs falling from the tables of the de Orrebys. He smiled in his sleep, hugging the small bolster of hay in memory of yesterday's adventures.

"Alditha. Alditha." He groaned as he whispered her name. Alditha Cherry was, at twelve years of age, five years younger than himself. But in experience she was old enough to be his mother. But then again, any daughter of Margaret Cherry was bound to know how the world revolved by the time she could know anything at all! He heard again that frivolous little laugh. The click of her tongue against pearl-white teeth as she beckoned. The rhythmic tap of her dainty toe as she feigned impatience . . .

The tap-tap-tap became bang-bang-bang and Jack shot upright in the darkened kitchen, still struggling with the dream. Someone was hammering on the door. And not the kitchen door, either. The main door of the Hall! That must mean visitors for the Master or Mistress! But who? At this time of night? Yawning, Jack ran both hands through his hair, scraping at his scalp in a effort to waken. He shivered as he pulled open the heavy, iron-studded door.

"Is Sir John at home?" The gruff voice of William Hesketh echoed round the empty hall as he pushed past the servant impatiently. His young squire, pale and hollow-eyed from hunger and lack of sleep, followed forlornly.

"He's abed, Sir. My Master was married today and I'd as soon not disturb him . . . " Jack wiped his nose on his sleeve in embarrassment. The visitor's servant managed a smile at that.

"Married? Grindon?" Hesketh sounded disbelieving. "Then may the moon be blue on the morrow! But then again . . ." He looked around the hall as Jack lit a couple of torches from the dying fire and returned them to the wall-sconces. "Isabel de Orreby, is it?" William chuckled. "Then he's earned himself a goodly slice of East Cheshire *and* kept up with the King for fashion! A devious man, your master, and no mistake." His laughter only turned to a bubbling cough when he heard the door of an upper room open.

"Who is it, Jack?" Jordon of Bolyn fastened the belt of a hurriedly donned woollen robe as he descended, his slim, boyish figure almost lost in its generous folds. He was bright and alert for, though it was well past midnight, sleep had been the furthest thing from his mind.

"William Hesketh. Here to see Sir John Grindon. If he can be interrupted . . ." The Lancashireman's plain features creased in a broad grin, the broken tooth at the front of his mouth bearing witness to his impetuous nature.

If he can be interrupted! The man could have no idea just how inconvenient the interruption was though he was obviously referring to the recent marriage. "William Hesketh." Jordon repeated the name sourly. "I'll tell Sir John you've arrived." He retraced his steps, annoyance showing in every movement. Why did this have to happen? Just what did he have to do to make any headway in his own little plans and schemes! He thought back to the week the King had visited Gawsworth Hall with his friend Piers Gaveston. A shudder went through him as he thought of that personable man now lying separated from his head, though the embalmers had no doubt made it look as though it had never been removed. And he remembered the night when Piers had sent for him to bring wine to his room. Jordon licked his dry lips as he opened the bedchamber door. Sir John lay as he had left him, his hands behind his head, tied tightly to a hook behind the bed and his ankles firmly secured to the bottom of the bed-frame.

"Someone called Hesketh has arrived." The boy tugged the rope free from his ankles and wrists, knowing that the ritual would have to wait. "Jack is getting them refreshments." He heard the resentment in his own voice. Gaveston had taught him many things, but patience was not one of them.

"Hesketh? What the devil does he want at this time of night!" John Grindon slipped his feet into a pair of soft shoes and shrugged on a robe. There had better be a good reason for getting a man out of bed in the middle of . . . the night.

In the kitchen Jack Sharpe plied a disgruntled Simon Bradford with bread, cheese and ale beside the warmth of the oven. "Wouldn't tomorrow have been soon enough?" He chewed on a crust companionably.

"When he has an idea he must put it into practice yesterday." Hesketh's squire tried to drown his melancholy in the ale. "He has been seized by the idea that there are perquisites to be had by those at the birth of a prince. He also gets it into his head that the child will be born within the hour! And him not there with his hand out."

"Then why come to Sir John?" Jack tried without success to find a connection.

"Because the bounty he seeks is the hand of Elbora de Totleworth."

"Elbora de Totleworth?" Jack was not one bit the wiser.

"Sole heiress to Richard de Totleworth. Sir John's cousin. On his mother's side."

"Oh." It was too much for Jack's brain.

"The Totleworth estates are vast and William Hesketh sees himself as a courtier, of a sudden. And as Sir John has the ear of the King already..."

"Hesketh! A courtier!"

"He also hopes some of Sir John's refinement will rub off on him, and he's in sore need of it! Rough as a hedgehog's arse, he is, though he wouldn't believe it himself. And changes his colours by the minute. With the King. Then with Lancaster. Now, back with the King. Whichever has the most to offer."

"Like many. Here, Sir John is for the King. His mother-in-law, married to a Fytton, must needs be with Lancaster and Robert Holland."

"And I go where I am bid. Right side or wrong. Win or lose." Simon slid once more towards melancholia.

"That's what comes of being well bred," Jack grinned mischievously. "Better to be common. And stupid. I make myself so useful about the kitchen and stables that they bid me stay here. Especially as I was never able to learn a proper skill. Hopeless with a bow. Worse with a sword. More of a hindrance than a help . . . "

"Crafty bastard." Simon could almost envy him that simple life.

"There's an idiot in every village, see." Jack stuck his thumb in his mouth to prove the point.

The door opened and Jordon of Bolyn stood there glowering, such anger in his black eyes that Jack shrank back against the wall on which he had been casually resting and Simon shivered uneasily.

"*You* ride at dawn!" The emphasis was on the first word, spat out viciously at the visitor. After all he'd done to advance himself he was being left behind! What *could* someone like himself do to rise above the mire they had been born in? He thought he'd done more than enough to buy John Grindon's affection, which only showed how wrong he could be! The man's excuse had been that the King and Court were at present playing happy families and waiting with bated breath for the birth of a prince. But that was not the reason. He was being abandoned. Probably in favour of some fresh-faced page in London Town. And without Sir John's contacts and manipulations on his behalf, how could he ever hope to become the great merchant who filled his dreams and every waking hour as well? He'd do anything, absolutely anything, to become a merchant. "Will you sleep in the kitchen, or share my bed?"

"I'd as soon stay here . . ." Simon managed to stutter.

"As you prefer." Jordon left them abruptly, his fists clenched and his mind seething.

"A wise choice," Jack nodded his head sagely. "Though he's in so foul a mood I doubt he would have bothered you."

But the ale had done its work and Simon was beyond thought. Sleep claimed him before he could question the remark so Jack, having one last scratch at his rump, curled up in his corner, clutched his bundle of hay and tried to return to his beloved Alditha.

In the bedchamber above the kitchen, sleep eluded John Grindon as he lay flat on his back gazing at the moonlit window-slit. Against the other wall, on the pallet usually occupied by the boy Jordon, William Hesketh snored loudly, expelled air whistling through the gap in his broken tooth. Where was Jordon now? He would be angry, and John was fully aware of the reasons. They had little to do with sentiment. That lad had a sharp brain in his head and would no doubt achieve his greatest ambition one day. The most important merchant in the Port of London. John could imagine him, strutting in his furs and chains, conducting his own affairs and everyone else's besides. And he'd use any means at his disposal to gain those ends, no matter what the personal cost. John swallowed the hard lump in his throat and choked back tears. There were always sacrifices to be made. Tonight he was the new owner of Gawsworth Hall. Today he had followed the trend the King had set. Well . . . almost. Because tonight he, John Grindon, was a married man, and he must leave Jordon behind.

As he stared at the night sky, a large silver star swooped to earth, trailing stardust in its wake.

"I wish . . . for Jordon to understand, one day, how much I have loved him. By the King's Grace . . . "

Gaveston's death and the imminent birth of the heir to the throne of England may have changed King Edward's allegiance temporarily, but sooner or later he would tire of playing the dutiful husband and look to his former friends. Sir John Grindon finally fell asleep one hour before the dawn only to be rudely awakened by his would-be cousin's hearty bellow.

★ ★ ★

Although the door was wide open to the light of the full moon it was warm amongst the familiar smells of hay and horse inside the stable. Geoffrey Bernulf moved his arm slightly without disturbing the woman now asleep, her head on his shoulder, her tears spent. He still couldn't believe it. This morning he had returned to Gawsworth in such high hopes, a jewel worth a fortune in his pocket and the firm conviction that Isabel de Orreby and the lands which should be his by ancestral right were within his grasp. He'd been on his way to her. And then Christiana, strolling to the wedding, had given him the news. Sir John Grindon! Courtier and friend of the King himself. The man who had once saved the life of Bernulf the Archer on a Scottish battlefield. Marrying Isabel de Orreby this very day! How could Fate play such a cruel trick?

Geoffrey listened to the steady breathing of the woman lying in his arms. Her face was pale in the moonlight, the shadows under her eyes accentuated by her almost ghostly pallor. Earlier he had seen her dressed in samite and velvet, a jewel at her throat and a ring on her finger, arm in arm with her husband as they left the church beside Gawsworth Hall. Old Edmund Fytton had conducted the service, the church having been newly licensed for the ceremony. Such was the influence of Grindon, once one of the

Prince's Pack under Piers Gaveston and still a man to be wary of, even in today's changing climate. Lancaster could be a very real threat to King Edward and there were those whose loyalty was doubtful. But Sir John was no turn-coat. And neither was Geoffrey Bernulf! So, though he hated the thought, they were destined to be always on the same side in a battle. It would have been much easier if the knight had been an enemy. Especially after the events of today.

He hadn't pushed her for an explanation. Isabel had been far too distressed to talk coherently. Entering the stable on his way to retrieve the ruby from the tunnel where he had hidden it, he had been astounded to find himself confronted by the bride, weeping as though the world had ended and dressed in a shabby old woollen gown more fitted to Petronilla, Isabel's maid.

"Love me. Just love me," she had sobbed.

And he had. Carefully and tenderly, with a depth of feeling neither had experienced in their lives before. They had slowly removed themselves from pain and disillusion, from heartbreak and shattered dreams, and found in one another a unity which both had long suspected but neither had expected to achieve. In their youth they had succumbed to lust and revelled in the secrecy of forbidden love. She could have lost her reputation and been sold to Christ for her sins. He could have lost his life! But he had always believed that one day there would be a way for him to claim her before the world. A way for him to be Master of Gawsworth Hall, owning the lands which had once belonged to his ancestor, Bernulf, a free man, whose ghost was said to haunt the stable yard beyond the door, where his cot once stood. But slowly he had seen her grow away from him. She had found other goals. Yearned for distant horizons. A different life. She had been given the chance to become a lady of the Court of Edward and Isabella and she had seized that chance gladly, riding away without so much as a backward glance at all his broken dreams. And somehow he had carried on his own life, paying dues to her as a tenant on her land, thatching to line his own pocket, poaching to line his stomach. And fighting for his King.

Geoffrey smiled to himself. She wasn't the only one to have met King Edward, either. Though he wouldn't dare tell anyone that he himself had been in such illustrious company. His Monarch had sworn him to secrecy though it was hardly necessary, under the circumstances. Who would ever believe that the King of England had once spent the biggest part of a day helping a local man to thatch a house in the middle of Macclesfield? Even if it was the most imposing house in town! They'd lock him away as a lunatic! No. Edward was no ordinary King, and that was probably at the bottom of his troubles with the Earls. They didn't understand him, looking always for a replica of his father, the first Edward, and never finding it. They took his gentleness as cowardice, his humanity for frailty, and his love of his fellow man for perversion. And by looking after his close friends, Edward had brought down on his own head the jealousy of the strongest men in England.

Isabel stirred, moving her face more closely into his chest and sighing in her sleep. Here was the biggest puzzle of all. She had spread her wings and flown. But she had regularly returned. She had openly spurned him, but the invisible thread which joined them had never been broken. The sight of her had always had his heart bursting from his breast, and he knew she felt the same. The colour in her cheek and the sparkle in her eye were always at odds with her imperious manner when she addressed him. Yet today she had married Sir John. She had denied the heart and followed the head on the very day he had returned with Piers Gaveston's ruby safely in his possession. And no one in the world knew he had it! Piers was dead only hours after handing it to him with the request that he beg the King to save his life. He should have taken it to the King anyway, he knew. But there was plenty of time. With those in power all at sixes and sevens with one another, it might prove prudent to hang onto the jewel for the moment. At least until he understood what had caused Isabel to run crying from her marriage bed into his arms, with no sign of a hue and cry over her disappearance. It was a complete mystery. And the minute she awoke he wanted the truth of it!

His gaze lingered on the soft square of half-light which he knew to be the open door. He saw, or imagined, a glisten of frost on the hard earth of the yard and felt beyond its open space to the rustling privacy of Three Mile Wood. Above the black, silhouetted trees the sky draped itself, a cloak of subtle grey across the forest. And then, from nowhere, a star blazed down, ripping through the stillness with a majestic power gathered in heaven, releasing its energy in a burst of light over those who watched.

"I wish . . ." Geoffrey hesitated for the fraction of a second. "I wish for my son to come to his rightful inheritance." His own attempts had so far proved futile. But his son *must* succeed.

"Oh . . . " Isabel moaned quietly, disturbed by his sudden indrawn breath. "What . . . ? Who . . . ? Oh. Geoffrey." She groaned as she said the name, realising where she was and the circumstances of being there. Sickness washed over her and clutching hard at his jerkin she gasped for air.

"I think you'd better tell me, hadn't you?" He kept his voice low and soothing, hoping she wouldn't begin crying again. Her eyes glistened with tears, but it was the profound misery in their emerald depths which moved him. Marriage had not lived up to her expectations.

"Tell you? How can I tell you? It's all my fault. It would have been better to have married that stunted dwarf Roger de Macclesfield than have brought this about. I'll never forgive myself. But worse. You will never be able to forgive me."

Roger de Macclesfield! Geoffrey hadn't given him a thought for years. He'd been betrothed to Isabel before that unfortunate accident! Though four foreigners who'd had the ill-luck to be in the woods at the time were hanged for the murder of the Runt, there was a lot Geoffrey the Poacher could have told the court on that law-day!

"Sir John must indeed be a poor lover if you now pine for de Macclesfield." He could not disguise the irony.

"Poor lover? Oh, God forgive me." Isabel turned her face into his shoulder as the tears began to seep through her lashes once more. "No lover at all to me. Or to any other woman on God's earth."

"What . . . ?" Geoffrey let out a low whistle. "No *woman* . . . ?"

Isabel released her hold on him and looked into his face, determined to confront the horror. "You say right. I felt very strange. All day. No. Not all day. Only from the moment I saw you take Christiana in your arms and kiss her with all the love you could muster. You smote me with a dagger. Drained the blood from me in a trice. How could you . . . ?"

"How could *I*? Ha! And you, the blushing bride, hanging on the arm of another man as you made ready to celebrate the nuptials. What was I supposed to do? Tear my hair and beat my breast in impotent rage? You should at least know me better than that."

"Oh, I do. Where did you take her? In the woods? Beside the river? Or did you savour your urges until you arrived back at the cot?" Jealousy sharpened her tongue; all the bitterness of the previous night surging back, causing her to strike out at the nearest to hand, even though that one was the one she loved.

Geoffrey understood. They had always lashed one another to a pulp, unable to compromise. She, the proud lady. He, the even prouder peasant. "Does it really matter? It's the way things are. The way things have always been. For more than fourteen years Christiana has been my bed-mate. For fourteen years she has waited with the patience of a saint for me to wed her. Did she rant and rail each time I wandered away in your direction, hoping like a fool to be given more than marching orders? Did she threaten to marry another when she knew for certain I would never love her as I loved you? So, yesterday, when I saw everything I had ever wanted taken from me by a man I *refuse* to hate, where would I turn?"

"A man you *refuse* to hate? Perchance after these happenings you'll have to change your mind." Isabel's voice had sunk to a whisper.

"My refusing to hate him has nothing to do with your disappointment in him as a lover. He persuaded you, for better or for worse. And you accepted him. For better or for worse . . ." He stroked her chestnut hair, gently removing a stray strand caught across her brow.

"And my disappointment and anger has nothing . . . *nothing* to do with his rejection of my body . . ."

"Nothing?" Geoffrey tilted her face towards him with a finger under her chin. Outside a blackbird began his morning song. Dawn was breaking. They would soon have to move or he'd have no choice in the matter of a fight with Mister Grindon.

"You must think me the most shallow of women to have run straight into your arms at such a moment. Am I so selfish and self-pitying that I can give no thoughts to anyone but myself?"

Geoffrey didn't answer. They'd both been selfish. Who was to say which had been the worse?

"It is more than that." She swallowed hard and he felt her tremble. "I was dazed. I could think of nothing but what you must be thinking. Of what you were doing. All through the feast your vision was before me. You and Christiana. So when he sent everyone away I thought nothing of it. When he escorted me himself to my room . . . my room! and undressed me with his own hands, I never questioned. Though I did wonder what had become of Petronilla and why the crowds were not hammering on the door to witness us abed . . . "

"And then? Am I to hear the sordid details?" Geoffrey wished he could just walk away. He didn't need this. He loved the woman and she had no right to torment him.

"And then he left me. Lying alone. I didn't understand. He said he was sorry . . . " Isabel twisted onto her knees, looking deep into her lover's eyes. "I heard them . . . "

"Them?" Now it was Geoffrey's turn to grasp at empty air for the truth.

"He had sent everyone away," Isabel repeated. "Everyone except Jordon."

Geoffrey didn't move a muscle. He just stared. She bit her lip hard as she saw him realise the implications.

"Jordon?" He grasped her so tightly by the shoulders that she felt the bruises form. "Jordon?" He screamed the word in disbelief. Jordon! Geoffrey Bernulf's only son. Raised by old Sybil until her death and then by Christiana. *She'd* loved him as her own. "My God. I'll kill him with my bare hands. I'll tear him limb from limb . . . " If he'd needed an excuse to hate Sir John Grindon, then he had one now.

Before Isabel realised what was happening he had thrust her from him and leaping to his feet was making for the stable door.

"Geoffrey! No! They'll hang you for sure!"

"Then they can hang me. But *he'll* meet his Maker before me."

He disappeared into the night leaving Isabel in a panic. She might have known he wouldn't stop to think! She might have guessed he would take the matter into his own hands.

"Oh, Geoffrey! What great fools we both are!"

But she couldn't let him do it alone. John Grindon was a fighting man despite his manicured nails and neatly shaped hair. His sword-arm was as strong as any and his agility on horseback renowned. He'd tilted and jousted and fought hand to hand with the best of them. Geoffrey was, first and foremost, an archer, and though he could skin an animal in moments with his dagger, against Sir John with his quick, calculating mind hiding behind deceptively soft grey eyes, he would stand little chance. Gathering her skirts up over her knees, her thick red-brown hair flowing loose almost to her waist, Isabel groped for the latch of the tunnel door. In his haste he had forgotten the tunnel. She could be inside the Hall before him.

"Mother of God, preserve me!" Jack Sharpe crossed himself fervently. He'd been about to open the tunnel door into the stable when it had vanished before his eyes, presenting instead a ghostly outline. Old Bernulf's spirit waited to enfold him!

"Jack? What on earth are you doing!" Isabel managed to retain some of her composure.

"Mistress?" Jack was even more

confused. What was Mistress Isabel doing in the stable at dawn, the morning after her wedding? He shook his head and pursed his lips. It was like he'd told that lad Simon Barford. The likes of them couldn't be trusted to wipe their own arses without help, so why follow them into battle? Only a madman would trust his Master with his life!

"I asked, what are you doing?"

"Obeying my Master, Mistress. I'm to get his horse immediately. Faster than immediately. He wants to be gone at dawn, and that was ten minutes ago."

"To be gone? Gone where? He said nothing of this to me." Mistress Grindon spoke to the servant as though he had lost the few faculties he had been born with.

"No . . . ?" Jack scratched his backside with one hand and his head with the other. His face brightened. "Perhaps he didn't want to wake you, Mistress. Mister Hesketh arriving so late, an' all."

"Mister Hesketh? You say Mister Hesketh arrived in the night?" She sighed. William was ever one to feather his own nest, but in trying to do so usually made enough commotion to raise the dead. What plan had he in his head now? Not Elbora de Totleworth again? "Then you'd best get the horse. And as quick as you can!" At least, she thought, Geoffrey was unlikely to tackle John and William together. And if John was riding off somewhere, all the better! It would give her handsome archer time to lay more circumspect plans.

The main hall of the house was empty as she cautiously entered, wary of being caught. The fire in the central hearth still glowed and wood-ash swirled and eddied in the draught from the open door. They were outside, awaiting Jack Sharpe.

Silently, she made her way to where three figures stood in the lightening morn. John Grindon, cool and calm, any hopes or fears expertly hidden behind the courtier's mask of elegance; William Hesketh, pacing impatiently, his breath steaming out in the cold air, his fingers flexing incessantly. And a youth; slim, pale and heavy-eyed who looked as though he'd rather be anywhere else than facing a long journey.

"Sir?" She bent her knee slightly to her husband, trying not to seek out the spot where Geoffrey Bernulf was most likely to be hiding.

"Mistress." John bowed his head, the shining cap of hair as immaculate as ever. "I had no wish to disturb you so early." Slowly he came towards her, taking in every perfect detail of her face. In the gentle light of a golden dawn it looked angelic. There it was again. That tightening of his rib-cage whenever he saw her like that. Virginal. Untouched. The image of his saintly mother. He wanted her to hold him. To caress him. To let him lay his head against the warm, inviting breast. And yet, last night when he had done just that, he had felt such revulsion at himself, such a sickness that he had fled from her, back to his own room. And Jordon.

"You are leaving?" It was obvious as Jack arrived up the slope leading John's horse.

John Grindon smiled. She could interpret his actions as she would. "For once, I fear Hesketh is right. It would be wrong planning to be away from the Court when the child is born. And of course I shall be making request to Queen Isabella that you resume your place in her retinue. But for the moment it is perhaps best that you take care of things here. I shall send for you soon. Very soon." Taking her hand in his he bent to kiss it.

Isabel didn't argue. He was running away. Why should he send for her? What interest could he have in her? He'd got what he wanted with the marriage. The house and the lands! What else had she to offer? He'd even taken Jordon . . .

As the three men rode away into the mists, Isabel sighed with relief. The horses had no sooner clattered across the bridge beside the lakes when Geoffrey appeared at her side.

"You'd best go help Tilda, Jack. It's bread day, isn't it?"

"Lor', Mistress! I'd forgot. She'll be up and about and scolding by this time, an' me not got the cart ready!" He whirled about on the ball of his foot like a spinning top and disappeared through the door into the house. The oven in the kitchen was used for meats and pies, but bread was baked in the bakehouse in Macclesfield; an occasion for good-wives to gather in the square of the town for a gossip, putting the world to rights and passing comment on those who failed to make appearance. Tilda hated being late. For one thing, she liked her loaves to have prime spot in the oven. And for another, every minute she loitered was a minute for the busy-bodies to discuss her shortcomings.

"Where's the lad?" Geoffrey's voice was cold and uncompromising.

"I haven't seen him since . . ." She shrank back. The man before her, black haired and black eyed, was suddenly all soldier. The gentle lover of an hour since nowhere in evidence. The furious peasant, ranting like a madman, submerged beneath an awesome determination.

"Don't kill him . . . !" Her voice seemed small and thin. He didn't hear her, brushing past her skirts into the house without another word.

A moment later, as Petronilla and her little daughter Benedicta arrived for a day's work at their Mistress's bidding, they were treated to the sight of Isabel Grindon, white-faced and trembling, watching Jordon of Bolyn being dragged from Gawsworth Hall by the strong silent arm of Geoffrey Bernulf.

"Mother of God, forgive me . . ." Isabel began to weep into her hands as she leaned against the wall, her legs seeming too weak to support her.

"Come inside, Mistress. You look worn out. Benedicta! Run to Tilda and tell her to prepare a tisane. And be quick! 'Tis bread day and she'll be gone in a minute."

Beside the still-warm hearth, Petronilla heard of the events of the previous night, tutting continuously like a mother hen comforting her young. For, although she knew her place, Petronilla Dane had shared all her Mistress's secrets in the past and between them was a bond defying class and status, though it remained largely undefined.

"Don't worry, Mistress. Bernulf may teach the boy the error of his ways, but he'll never harm a single hair of his only son's head." And she held the cup of hot liquid to Isabel's lips and Benedicta watched, wide-eyed.

* * *

"Sir John will have your life for this!" Jordon had given up trying to escape the iron grip.

"Sir John!" Geoffrey Bernulf spat a great gobbit of phlegm onto the path as he said his name. "May the very name rot your tongue, my lad. 'Twould have been better had I kept you here. Brought you up in my hovel with Christiana than have *him* get his misbegotten hands on you. Ideas above your station! And see where it has landed you!"

Jordon winced as his father's fingers bit more viciously into his flesh. But still he was his father's son. "Landed me! Ha! You think he raped me? Seduced me? The shoe was on the other foot!"

For these words Jordon received a stinging blow to the head.

"Whoreson! Turd!" Geoffrey seethed, stepping up the pace to prevent himself from doing the boy a fatal injury.

"*You* bait your traps in the woods. How else would you catch your reward? And so *I* baited mine in London Town." Jordon ducked as he saw the next blow coming. "And one day the gold of the Port of London will be mine!"

"Gold! What use gold when the Devil has your soul? I should have strangled you at birth rather than have risked death as I did . . ."

"Risked death?" Jordon managed to gasp. He was out of breath after the two-mile chase along the lanes.

No explanation of those words was forthcoming as at that moment they arrived at the door of a cottage, clean and attractive, nestling in a small hollow at Lane Ends.

"Well, Geoffrey. What a surprise." Margaret Cherry's voice was husky with warmth and overflowing with welcome. "And Jordon. What fine velvets young gentlemen of the King's Court do wear!"

She stepped aside, allowing them to enter. Only then did the archer release his grip on the bruised breathless boy.

"Ignore the trappings, Mistress. At dawn today I learned that I had spawned a sodomite. And if you can teach him another path then you'll have meat in your bellies till twelve months come Candlemas."

"Oh, such a waste, Chuck." She ruffled Jordon's black curls, laughing softly at the challenge Geoffrey had presented her with. "But between us, I don't doubt we can change your ideas of pleasure. Alditha!" She beckoned her young daughter forward.

Jordon's fear of punishment at his father's hand had turned to acute embarrassment and he squirmed a little as his face reddened under scrutiny. Mistress Cherry was a buxom woman, with full breasts and ample, rounded hips, her manner so cheerful and affectionate that she might almost have been the ideal mother. The mother he had never known. Christiana had fed him and kept him clean when he was small, but he knew she had never loved him. Not as a mother would have loved him. Something had always held her back, though what that something was he could never discover. He knew instinctively that Margaret Cherry had enough love to encompass half the county and a tremor, half fear, half hope, ran through him.

Alditha was different. She was around his own age. Twelve or thirteen, he guessed. And the hair, allowed to cascade over her shoulders in virginal splendour, was the colour of honey. She was as slim as her mother was plump and as shy as her mother was fulsome, the smile on her lips so chaste that the young squire would have sworn she was a novice at such games. Her eyes, he noticed before she modestly lowered her lids, were the same light-brown as hazelnuts, and the look she gave him in that moment played havoc with the normal steady beating of his heart.

Geoffrey Bernulf watched his son's face turn from white to red and back to white and he smiled at Mistress Cherry who winked broadly in return. The boy was not beyond redemption.

★ ★ ★

Jordon of Bolyn gently touched the soft, creamy-white skin of the girl lying naked beside him and the thrill of youthful passion turned in seconds to a throbbing, aching desire. She opened her sleepy eyes, smiling.

"Again, my love?"

And as he slid once more into the silken, pulsating warmth that was Alditha, he thanked Mistress Margaret from the bottom of his heart for her tenderly administered lessons of yesterday.

2

SWEAT? Or shiver? It seemed there could be no happy medium but Isabel knew she simply had to get away from the claustrophobic atmosphere of the Queen's apartments or make a fool of herself by fainting. Seventeen-year-old Isabella of France could only be admired for her fortitude! The first cramps had begun during the previous night but even now, half-way through the afternoon, she had not made a single complaint, not given way to a single groan, and still walked the floor for exercise although the birthing stool had been ready for days. Isabel remembered her mother giving birth to Richard, John Fytton's eldest son. It had opened her eyes to the grotesque, primitive functions women were forced to perform before others, whether it be neighbours intent on helping, or courtiers witnessing that the child was indeed that of the Queen. She shuddered, both with cold and disgust, making her way through the crowded corridors to a part of the building where she could find time to breathe. The stone walls were giving off the musty smell left over from a damp autumn and Isabel longed to be back home. Briefly she wondered whether her husband would take up John Fytton's plan to build a new Hall at Gawsworth, lower down the slope, beside the lakes . . .

Judging by the assortment of objects littering the small anteroom, it had fallen out of general use some time ago. There were one or two broken pieces of armour and a cracked iron cauldron, a table which seemed to have been ablaze before being abandoned, and a great stuffed eagle, wings spread to accommodate the maximum number of fleas, and losing a feather each time the door opened. The view from the window was not towards the river but out over the huddle of buildings with the smells and noise of a thousand inhabitants. Isabel stood, not seeing the chaos, but scanning the horizon where parkland and forest provided the Royal household with hunting.

"How different from the dream is the

reality." She sighed as she spoke.

"Aye. If only we could wake and find reality the dream!"

Isabel nearly jumped out of her skin as she turned. She could have sworn that she was alone.

"I'm sorry. I didn't mean to startle you."

Margaret de Clare, widow of Piers Gaveston, Earl of Cornwall, sat quietly on an old chair, the back of which had been broken into jagged splinters. In the shadows of the jumbled pieces she was almost invisible.

"Still no child?" Margaret's voice was devoid of emotion.

"Isabella still paced when I left not many minutes ago. She has courage, you have to admit."

"A commodity we can scarce live without in this place." A note of bitterness crept into the young woman's tone.

Isabel drew up a mildewed cushion to sit on as she leaned against the wall. She smiled sadly. The truth about her own marriage to Sir John had been difficult to accept, but how much more difficult had Margaret de Clare's marriage been with the King's enemies accusing Piers of 'enticing our lord the King to do evil in various deceitful ways'. The most frequently referred to being 'the unnatural fornication between men'. And through it all, Margaret de Clare, sister of Gilbert, Earl of Gloucester, had managed to walk proudly with her head high. But privately, Isabel knew, she had seethed.

"At least Edward has seen fit to do his duty." Margaret raised a questioning eyebrow at her companion. "And how is marriage to Sir John?" There was the hint of a smile at the corner of her pretty mouth. Margaret was the second eldest of Gilbert's three sisters, Eleanor being the older and Elizabeth younger, but she was acknowledged as being the most handsome. Superficially the sisters were very much alike, but Margaret's eyes were just that fraction bigger, her nose just slightly finer, and her lips had just a hint more fullness. These tiny variations made all the difference.

Isabel shivered again in the November chill. "Sir John . . ." Her voice trailed away miserably.

"I know." Margaret leaned forward

and patted her hand. "I know. Piers and Sir John were friends before your husband ever went to Langley. Before the King had ever heard the name of Grindon." She nodded knowingly. "But what say have we in these matters? Marriages are arranged and take little account of *our* preferences."

"You should have told me!" Isabel could hardly believe it. "My marriage wasn't arranged at all. My previous husband was murdered. My father and my brother were dead. Sir John just . . . happened to be there."

"How fortunate for Sir John," Margaret quipped sarcastically.

Mistress de Clare was right. John Grindon had manoeuvred himself into a position of authority at Gawsworth, and manipulated her with no difficulty at all. Now everything she had inherited belonged to him. Worse. *She* belonged to him. And there was nothing she or Geoffrey Bernulf could do about it.

"You really didn't know?" Margaret was amazed. "Any of it?"

"Why should I?" Isabel asked. "I know men in Cheshire who have fought by the

King's side. They have lived with him on battlefields, seen him wield his sword, seen him kill . . . Not once have they witnessed anything to prove the rumour put about by Lancaster . . . "

Margaret lowered her voice to a whisper. "I well knew my husband's winning ways and I confess there is no proof that rumour says true. Edward was foolish. But more than that I cannot say. He gave Piers everything he wanted, though whether he went so far as to love him in the flesh, I know not. Piers had squires aplenty to gratify those appetites . . . "

"They stayed a week at Gawsworth Hall . . . " Isabel thought back to that time. "And you are right. Now that I remember. It was Gaveston and Grindon who kept company. The King remained for the greater part looking to the running of the estate and poking into this and that. Visiting cottages and talking to my peasants."

"That's our Majestic King all right! He'd as soon be building a wall as governing England! As I said. More foolish than wicked."

"But then, haven't we all been foolish in our time?" Isabel reminded her. "When I first came to Court, ignorant and rustic, I was overwhelmed by the elegance and confidence of the young women, yourself included. I saw you coy and flirtatious with the courtiers . . . At least, with those in the Prince's Pack, which numbered both Gaveston and Grindon amongst its members."

"Ah. We were but children, feeling first lust and not understanding the things we saw. Piers Gaveston was the most eligible of all, being the Prince's closest friend. It was as near as we could get to becoming Queen! It was a game. Nothing more."

"Games. 'Tis all a game of chance. Look at Alice. In a passion at having to marry an old man, but at least she *got* a man!"

"Alice? Alice de Lacy? Aye." Margaret began to giggle. "One she'd as soon be without." Seeing the puzzled expression on Isabel's face she explained. "He's more soldier than man and uses her only as he would a casual whore. Two minutes thresh and thrust and it's all over. Alice pines for romance. For kisses.

And caresses. She longs for a man who can pleasure her, for Thomas Lancaster never will! And being in his thirty-sixth year, I think it too late for him to learn new lessons."

"Oh." Isabel sounded saddened. "Then there is no one content with their lot."

"Mayhap the Queen . . . "

"Now she has the King's undivided attention . . . "

"Now she has the heir to the throne . . . "

"Faith, I hope not. Sir John will be more than angry if the event has taken place and his wife not in attendance!" Isabel scrambled to her feet. "And should you not . . . ? For your brother's sake?"

Within minutes the two women had made their way back to the Queen's apartments to find that the event was imminent.

Isabella was at last astride the birthing chair, sweat beading her pale brow, her breath catching raggedly in her throat, and a dozen men, selected by the King, staring at the distended belly, the widespread legs strapped tightly to the sloping struts, and the area of thickly matted pubic hair.

"Push!" Mistress Leygrave instructed.

Isabel watched the varying expressions on the faces of the watching men. Some lusted. Some found sadistic pleasure. Some thanked God they had been born men. All viewed the young girl's labours with intense fascination and as Isabel saw pain glaze Queen Isabella's eyes she knew their patience would soon be rewarded. They were about to hear her scream.

Half an hour later an exhausted Isabella was placed, weak and bloody, into her sick-bed. There she would remain for fourteen days being fed gruel and purgatives to clear her body of the evil humours caused by childbirth, except for the morrow, when she would be carried on a litter to the chapel to give thanks for her safe delivery.

"Sweet Isabella. I am the happiest man alive." King Edward, twelve years senior to the young Queen, had tears in his eyes. "Never have I witnessed such a miracle as seeing my son born. Edward. A lucky name for kings, I think, as I was the fourth of my father's sons yet came to inherit the crown. What say you?"

"As you wish, my lord." Isabella lowered her lids respectfully.

"And this shall be our new beginning. Before long the palace will be overflowing with princes and princesses. Listen!" There was the sound of cheering from outside and a red glow lit the sky as celebration fires were kindled in the town. The feasting had begun. Edward bent to kiss Isabella's brow. "The people are well pleased with their Queen."

The chosen courtiers too seemed pleased, though at the mention of a new beginning and the thought of hordes of children of the marriage, one or two could be seen exchanging worried glances. There were those amongst the company who had treasured hopes of slipping into Gaveston's vacated chair. This newly formed emotional bond between King and Queen could only interfere with such plans.

"And my wife shall have her reward. Whatever you wish, Isabella. If it be in my power." Edward waited expectantly.

It was then that the young girl, tired, lonely and still suffering the pains of childbirth, reminded her husband that she was a Princess of France. The bright blue eyes were suddenly wide open, determined, and demanding. "I would like the return of my jewels, Husband. That is all." And she sank back, trembling, into the softness of the feather pillow.

Edward remained perfectly still, the only movement, a muscle twitching in his neck. But when he spoke his voice was clear and controlled. "My dear, you shall have them." And turning abruptly he left the chamber.

"She's either brave or stupid," Margaret whispered to Isabel. "Fancy reminding him of that at a time like this!"

All Isabella's jewels had been given, piece by piece, to Gaveston and, apart from the items carried habitually on his person, were now in the possession of Thomas of Lancaster. The Queen was asking that he gave her back the love-tokens he had showered on his friend. But not the love with which they had been given. She had been too humiliated. Tolerance was all she had to offer for the future.

Before the great banquet Sir John Grindon and his lady paid homage to the King, presenting him with a gift to his new-born son, a silver acorn set with sapphires which Sir John had decided was worth going into debt for.

"We thank you." The King had said the words a hundred times already and the queue seemed to grow rather than diminish. Then he noticed Isabel. Still carrying with her that strange aura of virginity. Yet . . . "And do you find marriage to your liking, Mistress?" Edward held out his hand for her to kiss.

"Sir John is as kind and gentle a husband as I could ever wish for," Isabel murmured.

"And enriched by those pretty Cheshire estates." The King smiled at John Grindon. "I remember the place with affection. But what of the boy? Jordon. I have missed him about the Court during the celebrations. He is not ill?"

Isabel was startled that the King should think to ask. "No, Sire. He is at Gawsworth, helping to administer the estate in my husband's absence."

"Ah, yes. He had ambition in the field of commerce. And if memory serves me right, on a warm day in Macclesfield I made a promise that I would see he had his chance..." For a moment Edward was again sitting with the thatcher... what was his name? Bernulf! That was it! Watching him hammer home the pegs in the roof. "Have him come to Court. Soon. I think when we visit my wife's family in France, he may accompany us. In the spring."

★ ★ ★

"So he married you!" Avelina Boundle had had it in her head for years that her cousin John was not the marrying kind. Her eyes had almost popped from her round face when she had heard the news. "And again presented you to the King!" It was the most aggravating thing! Here she was. On the doorstep of the Royal Residence, and related to a knight, and never been presented! How she could have lorded it over the neighbourhood if John had been more amenable to the suggestion!

"I have but a minor place." Isabel knew that Mistress Boundle would give all her teeth for such a minor place. "But I was present at the birth." She waited as the words fell into silence.

"Birth! Present at the birth! Oh." She sat down as though her legs had given way, her plump backside hanging over both sides of the narrow chair.

"I am not inconveniencing you in any way?" Isabel smiled sweetly. She had lodged with Avelina on the other occasions she had visited London and knew well the answer.

"What a ridiculous idea! Inconvenience? Never." Avelina recovered her wits. "Angareta! Where is that girl?" She called again. "Angareta!"

Her ten-year-old daughter emerged from the kitchen, ash from the fire smutting her face and her arms wet up to the elbows.

"Yes?"

"Yes, Mother! Will you never learn manners? And haven't you finished scouring yet? Lor', girl. If you didn't spend so much time dreaming of handsome young men carrying you away to

Paradise you'd have done it in half the time. Bring my special jar. And two cups." Mistress Boundle wanted all the details of the new Prince's entrance into the world, and a cup or two of her honey liquor would be sure to do the trick.

"It is very good of you." Isabel pretended that the welcome was unexpected. "And though I hate myself for it, I have a very great favour to ask. It does rather presume friendship between us."

"Presume? What *do* you mean? Of course we are friends! How else could it be otherwise when you are married to my cousin. We are better than friends. We are *family* . . . Isabel."

"Why, thank you, Avelina. And thank you, Angareta." Isabel took the cup of proffered liquid from the girl. "What lovely eyes your daughter has." Angareta's eyes were enormous in her thin face and of a strangely haunting colour. Almost blue. Almost grey. The colour being embellished with tiny specks of silver. Angareta smiled shyly and bobbed a curtsey. It wasn't often she received a compliment.

"Aye. She takes her better points from

me. And her brains from her father, God rest his soul." Widowhood had made something of a martyr of Mistress Boundle though there were those who thought Robert Boundle's disappearance at sea from a trade-ship which arrived safely, something of an act of providence. "But what favour?" She couldn't help feeling smug.

"Where I live, in Cheshire, there is a young squire, Jordon of Bolyn, son of a man living on my land. The boy is clever . . . " Isabel paused, building the suspense. "And he has come to the King's notice."

"How so? How, to the King's notice?" Avelina was on the edge of the seat, threatening to upturn it with the imbalance of her weight.

"I cannot tell you." They had all sworn that they wouldn't tell of the King's visit to Gawsworth. "Except that he has been to London on a previous occasion, in the company of my husband, Sir John."

"Ah." Avelina's chins quivered as she nodded.

"All I can say is that yesterday King Edward asked my husband to bring the boy to Court in order that he may travel with the Royal party to France in the spring. And . . . " Again Isabel allowed a small silence. "And I feel he would be in safe hands lodging within these walls."

"Ah." Once more the chins quivered as Avelina pondered. Was this woman, with all the elegance and refinement of a true lady, telling her that her suspicions about Sir John were true? Or was she simply showing a natural concern for the welfare of a young uneducated country bumpkin at the mercy of the town of London?

"My dearest Isabel, it will be a pleasure." Avelina patted the other woman's hand in a gesture of affection, adding as an afterthought, "Is he clean?"

Isabel smiled inwardly. What ideas these Londoners nurtured about their northern counterparts. "I shall make sure of it before I allow him to travel," she assured the anxious landlady.

★ ★ ★

Jack Sharpe sat beneath the gibbet at the corner of Gallows Field, sobbing his heart out, the hem of his smock stuffed in his mouth like a baby with its comfort-bib. Every so often he reached up to hit out at the foot-bones of the whitened skeleton above him, setting them swinging and rattling in the afternoon light. He'd lost her. She'd never look at him now that Jordon of Bolyn had taken a fancy to her.

"Ohhh. Alditha. Alditha." The words were muffled through the cloth. Then he hit the skeleton so hard that the left foot spun off into the road before splintering into its several components.

"Desecration!"

The voice seemed to thunder at him from the skies and Jack cringed down automatically, awaiting blows. Nothing happened. Slowly he turned his head to see two young gentlemen on horseback staring at him.

"Mister Richard, Sir. Mister Hugh." Jack put his hand to remove his cap, only to find that he wasn't wearing one. Scrambling to his feet be bowed his head instead to John Fytton's sons by Cecily, Mistress Isabel's mother.

Richard Fytton, fifteen years old had, in common with the rest of his family, little respect for man or beast, saving only horse-flesh. His brother, two years younger, took a rather more aesthetic view of life.

"'Tis easy enough to pick a fight with the brigand's bones. But if you're looking for a real one . . . " Richard Fytton grinned at the simpleton wickedly.

"I am, Sir. That I am!" Jack was as emphatic as he could be.

"Then shall we take you on for tuppence? One at a time? Or can you beat us both at once?"

"Oh, no, Sir. 'Tis not you or Mister Hugh I'd like to fisticuff." He sniffed loudly and wiped his nose on his arm.

"Then who?" Richard leaned forward, smiling. "Tell us and we'll truss him for you."

"I was on my way to Lane Ends to see Alditha and as I passed the spinney I heard her laugh. I thought she'd seen me, Sir and that it was her way of calling me, so I went into the trees . . . " His temper got the better of him again and he lashed out at the brigand, sending a shin bone after the foot. "And there she was. Merry as you please, being tumbled by Jordon of Bolyn! The girl I thought I would marry. I thought she would have me. I thought . . . " He lapsed into silence, crest-fallen and miserable. He stood no chance against Jordon. Jordon had fine clothes and lived upstairs. Jordon had been to London. Jordon could read and knew how to reckon . . . It wasn't fair!

"Jordon of Bolyn? With Alditha Cherry?" Richard whistled. "My, my! But that's a new turn of events!"

"He does it for spite, I shouldn't wonder," Hugh murmured. "Sir John leaving him behind . . . "

"But he must be keen, to try her in the spinney. Even a fine day in January is cold when your arse is bare. Don't worry, Jack. We'll have him beg your forgiveness before nightfall."

They'd been on their way from their father's house in Macclesfield to their sister's house in Gawsworth having received a message that she had recently arrived back from Court. But a diversion was always welcome. Especially one involving that upstart foundling, Jordon of Bolyn! It was well known he'd only attained his place by sodomy, leaving those who should by rights have ridden with Sir John fuming and looking for mischief around the lanes of Cheshire. The Fytton brothers were not averse to a little revenge.

★ ★ ★

There were more ways than one of skinning a cat, Jordon decided. His breath steamed out before him and his feet crunched the hardening ridges of mud as he walked happily home. He would be eternally grateful to his father, though when necessary he would not hesitate to use the same means to gain an advantage. Whatever he did was not for momentary gratification, but for profit. Excepting Alditha, of course . . .

An ambush was the last thing he was expecting. One minute he was striding out, alone on the edge of Three Mile Wood, and the next he was fighting for his life. If they hadn't taken him by surprise he could have overcome them, he was sure, but with his head inside what felt and smelt like a horse blanket, he had no chance at all. Jordon struggled until he was exhausted and almost suffocated, waiting for the final blow. It never came. Before too many minutes had passed he realised that they were not trying to take his life, but his clothes! Every stitch was stripped from him, then he was gagged and blindfolded and hung by his arms from what he could only guess was the branch of a tree. Throughout the operation, his assailants uttered not a word. So, he reasoned, he must know them. They kept dumb so that he could not recognise them. But who were they? And why strip him? One was bigger than either himself or the other thief. And stronger. And rougher. Then they were gone, on horseback, in the direction he himself had been heading. And he was hanging like a plucked goose in a cool-room, waiting to be drawn and stuffed.

Jack Sharpe stood looking at the stark naked figure as it writhed and wrestled with the ties around its wrists. Sucking his thumb he stared in fascination at the muscle in shoulder, belly and thigh. This body had defiled Alditha. This body had raped the girl of his dreams. This body was in pain . . . Jack turned away. He didn't like to watch anything in pain. Not even animals. Not even creepy crawlies living in the walls of his corner by the oven. Jordon of Bolyn was hurting and it would be best if he just left him there and went home.

Ralph Dane was on his way home, hand in hand with his daughter Benedicta, listening to her non-stop chatter and thinking how like her mother she was becoming. Petronilla had sent her to fetch him to his supper and the child had kept up the stream of information without seeming to stop for breath.

"And did you know that Dickon Miller's wife, Mistress Maud, had a new baby only the other day? Another girl, an' her so badly wanting a son. Mother says she'll be having babes till she drops to have a boy after yesterday's news . . . You did hear yesterday's news, didn't you?" Benedicta looked up at her father.

"No. But I expect you'll tell me," Ralph grinned.

"Dickon's mother, who married Tom Helesby after the miller died, an' him only half her age, has had a boy herself! Now what do you think of that? Disgusting, Mother said . . . "

"Almost a miracle, I should think," Ralph chuckled. What Tom had ever seen in the toothless hag was beyond understanding. How he'd ever managed to get her with child was one of the wonders of the world!

"What was that?" Benedicta stopped, pulling her father to a halt. "I thought I heard something. Just in the wood. Over there." She pointed.

"Let's see then. It could be a rabbit caught in one of Bernulf's traps." Ralph was not above helping himself to Geoffrey's catch now and again, if the opportunity presented itself. It didn't sound like a rabbit. More like bigger game. Hog. Or a small deer perhaps, by the creaking of the branch, though Bernulf was slipping in his ways to put a trap so near to the lane that it would be discovered.

"Oh. Oh." Benedicta found words failing her for once as she gazed in horror on the naked form of Jordon of Bolyn, his arms almost wrenched from their sockets by his efforts to free himself, scratches on his pale skin oozing blood where nearby branches had pierced his flesh.

"Well, here's a pretty sight!" Ralph couldn't help laughing as he wrapped his arms around the lad's thighs, lifting him to take the weight from his aching arms. In seconds the shepherd had Jordon on his feet, the gag removed and the blindfold pulled from his eyes. "Much longer and you'd have either twisted yourself into a knot or frozen to death. And who wanted to put a stop to your antics, might I ask?"

"They came at me from behind . . ." Jordon shivered as he rubbed at his scarred wrists. "Two of them. Well . . . at least two. And if I ever find out . . . !"

"Here." Ralph Dane wrapped his sheepskin jerkin round the boy's shoulders. "Before you shake yourself to pieces. It doesn't cover much of your modesty, mind, but I'm sure Benedicta won't look too hard." He chuckled. His daughter hadn't taken her eyes from Jordon of Bolyn and she must know him, blemishes and all, from head to toe by now. Benedicta blushed, still tongue-tied, but having the grace to lower her gaze to the ground.

"I'll kill them . . . " Jordon was having trouble speaking through chattering teeth.

"Save your strength," Ralph advised. "Come on, lad. It isn't far to my cottage and you can borrow some of my old clothes to get you back to the Hall in a decent manner. And no doubt Petronilla will feed you before she lets you go."

★ ★ ★

"I don't know what the world is coming to," Petronilla grumbled. Jordon had left with a belly-full of pea-dollop and a set of clothes three sizes too big for him. "Things weren't so bad when we were young. In those days it was safe to walk the lanes hereabouts . . . "

"Try telling that to Roger de Macclesfield." Ralph yawned. His wife had fixed ideas and he knew from experience that it was a waste of breath arguing with her. Benedicta was usually the same. But not tonight. The girl had other things on her mind. She must be growing up!

"That was different. Roger de Macclesfield

was murdered by foreigners. Some of their bones still hang on the gibbet. Whoever strung Jordon up knew him. You can be sure of that."

"It's not surprising. Not many approve of *that* kind of behaviour round here. Nor anywhere I shouldn't think."

"Not his father, that's for certain. And from what I hear the lad's changed his ideas now anyway, thanks to Alditha Cherry." Petronilla said the name scathingly. It was many years now since she had found her suspicions regarding Ralph and Margaret Cherry proved. On one occassion, at least. There could have been more. It irked her that Alditha had the self-same honey coloured hair as Benedicta. It was a thorn in her side. Was she . . . ? Or wasn't she? Petronilla could never be sure.

"Come here, vixen. Don't rake up the past." Ralph gave her the benefit of that half-teasing smile. It was as well not to let a woman be too certain of herself. A little mystery kept her from straying. And she was still an attractive woman.

These thoughts were confirmed a moment later as a confident knock on the door heralded the arrival of a visitor.

"Don't tell me I'm late for supper! I've travelled what feels like a thousand miles in a single day just for a taste from Mistress Dane's spoon!" Adam Banaster, his tangerine-coloured hair as wild and extrovert as its owner, stood on the threshold, arms outstretched, expecting a joyous welcome.

"You'll get more than a taste of the spoon! It will be a box round the ears from my ladle if you tread filth onto my floor!"

Ralph grinned as his wife began her tirade against his cousin. She had never taken to him though over the years he had used all his charm and persuasion to seduce her. Quite openly. And only half in fun. "So apart from enjoying the spectacle of my wife roused in temper, what brings a Lancashire man to Cheshire?"

"Trouble! You can be sure of it!" Petronilla mumbled to herself.

"Lack of trouble!" But Adam tapped the side of his nose to admit to more than he was saying, glancing at Benedicta's quiet form in the corner. She had curled into a ball, still thinking her own thoughts, and fallen asleep.

"She'll not listen," Ralph told him as he brought out some of his wife's best ale. "She's dreaming of things for her future, I shouldn't wonder."

"Poor child." Petronilla well remembered herself at that age. Desperate to attract Ralph Dane, yet frightened of giving in to his obvious needs. It had been the example of Margaret Cherry that had sent her finally into his arms when he came back from the war with Scotland.

Having settled by the hearth and taken his first gulp of ale, Adam Banaster told them something of the world outside.

"I came from London with Robert Holland, a town where they talk a lot and do very little. The Queen demands her jewels. Lancaster had them, but has more on his mind than a few baubles."

"A few baubles? Ha! A King's ransom, no doubt!" Mistress Dane tried to imagine jewels fit for a Queen and failed.

"And were they in my hands instead

of Lancaster's, I should adorn you with every one." Adam never missed an opportunity.

"More on his mind, you say?" Ralph was leaning forward eagerly.

"There is word that Robert the Bruce is using King Edward's sudden urge to play no other role than dutiful husband to gain back some of his former holdings. Edward is in no mood to listen. And I wouldn't mind a wager to say that Isabella's *trinkets*," he smiled at Petronilla, "will be put to good use should Thomas need an army."

"But they've overcome their difficulties . . . " Ralph had understood them to be on the same side again.

"The King and Lancaster will never see eye to eye. For the moment, maybe. But Holland and the Fyttons are even now up at the Hall deciding on a pact for the future."

"Are the Scots not enemy enough that the English must fight amongst themselves?" Petronilla could not imagine that her husband would ever side against the King in any argument. No more than would Geoffrey Bernulf, or Dickon

Miller, or Tom Helesby, or Edgar Bagulay...

"Aye. There can only be one King." Ralph drained his cup.

"One King, aye. But which man is best fitted to be King? That's the question. No one can pretend that Edward is half the man his father was. Old Edward was a soldier to his toenails." Adam was staring at his cousin seriously, his usual cheery veneer discarded for a moment. "And you can't deny that Lancaster is of royal blood, being Edward's cousin and both being grandsons of the old King Henry."

"But Lancaster's father was but the second son. No. Edward is the true King and can never be other." Ralph saw the situation as an immovable object. The King was the King. How could any other presume to take a title conferred as a birthright?

"Then we must sit twiddling our thumbs while the Bruce takes all our northern holdings. Those castles our comrades died to capture. Remember our friend Jordon Marton? The battle of Falkirk? Did he lose his brains at the age of eighteen for nothing? Do we say to Bruce 'Come, take all you wish. We are content to play peek-a-boo with baby for a while'?" Adam pushed his hands through his fiery locks until they stood on end. "I can't stand inactivity! A man must be doing! Time to sit and suck his gums when he is in his dotage!"

"The King's no coward, if that is your meaning." Ralph was quick to his monarch's defence. "You've fought with him. You know he is a swordsman as good as any. He led us fearlessly at Kildrummie and came away drenched in Scottish gore . . . "

"Aye. But they were his father's plans. He but followed orders. Where are the orders now? That is where he fails. He is too interested in babes and banquets, and the new method for building in the south. He speaks with peasants about their work and puts more thought into the disposal of slops than into battle-plans. And the men he has closest to him are there to discuss the latest tune written for three gitterns and a harp! Half prefer their young squires to their wives . . . "

"Not the King!" Ralph Dane was on

his feet protesting, the sight of young Jordon of Bolyn, stripped and hung, fresh in his mind. "There are always those who wallow in depravity. You've witnessed it the night before a battle! Men hell-bent on pleasure, no matter who with, in case it be their last. But not Edward! And anyone saying so is a liar paid by Lancaster!"

"Paid by Lancaster, aye." Adam Banaster narrowed his eyes. "And have you forgotten? So are you! Since Lincoln chose to stop breathing, Lancaster, through little Alice de Lacy, is Earl of Chester too! I should have a care, cousin." The words were menacing.

"'Tis no wonder there are wars when men can quarrel over nothing." Petronilla thought it time to put an end to the evening. "Aren't we all English when all comes to all? Great loons, the pair of you, and nothing to choose between for common sense! If women ruled . . ."

"Then take me in hand, Mistress. How many times do I have to beg?" Adam consciously pushed his politics aside. This was neither the time nor the place. But he would remember . . . He reached out towards Petronilla playfully, only to get his knuckles rapped by her wooden spoon.

For once, Ralph Dane couldn't laugh at the by-play. Adam Banaster had been turning up on the doorstep unannounced for years. Now he asked himself why. Not that he didn't trust Petronilla. She gave his cousin nothing but the rough edge of her tongue. But there was more to the man than first met the eye. And Mister Dane the shepherd, archer to the Manor of Gawsworth, decided at that moment that his hospitality would not be quite so warm in the future.

★ ★ ★

Jordon had no wish to become a laughing stock. The Fyttons were rough and crude at the best of times and at the moment, John Grindon being away, the place was crawling with them. Cecily Fytton insisted on chaperoning her daughter at the slightest excuse, Gawsworth Hall, her home for years during her first marriage to Isabel's father, holding most of her memories. He made use of the tunnel.

John Fytton had talked of such big plans on his wedding night! A new Hall, down beside the lakes. And a tunnel joining it to the old Hall. There had been many knowing looks and nods at that! The tunnel had been constructed, but the new Hall was still a dream. Stealthily he crept past the kitchen and up the back stair to the tiny gallery above, keeping well into the shadows as he looked down from his vantage point into the main hall below.

On the raised dais beyond the central hearth, John Fytton lounged casually in his chair as though he was still Master of Gawsworth. His brother Hugh, horn cup in hand, sat beside him on a wooden settle, while Thomas, wildest of the three, concentrated on sharpening his dagger on a piece of stone. They were deep in earnest discussion, but the only words Jordon could make out were 'Lancaster', 'Edward', and 'Bruce'. They were obviously wondering about another campaign to Scotland in the spring.

Sitting on the hearth, their shoes almost in the ashes, were John Fytton's two sons, Richard and Hugh, half-listening to their elders, and half making their own conversation as they roasted turnips on the embers. Every few minutes the youngsters burst into laughter, only stifling the noise when father or uncle looked their way. Jordon turned to go, intending to take off the ridiculous clothes borrowed from the shepherd. They stank of peasant sweat and sheep shit. Below him, the kitchen door opened and Jack Sharpe could be seen making his way carefully towards the group carrying a heavy jug of liquor. Jordon hesitated. He watched as the men were served and Jack turned to leave.

"Here, Jack." Richard Fytton beckoned the lad. "Did you relieve the turd of his vitals? Or is he still alive and freezing?"

Poor Jack looked behind him anxiously, terrified of anyone knowing he was implicated. What would happen when Sir John found out? There'd be new bones at the corner of Gallows Field and no mistake!

"Stop shaking, you great idiot. Nothing can happen to you. Sir John has gone to the King, and when Lancaster takes the throne *we'll* be with *him*, won't we?

And Sir John will suffer the same fate as . . ."

He faltered as his father interrupted. "Have you no brains in your head? I've a mind to cut out your tongue . . . Here, Thomas! Your dagger!" He held out his hand to his brother. Richard shrank back, burning his hand on a hot ash as he did so.

"Ow!" He yelled at the pain.

"Serves you right, you foetid whoreson! You'll have us all to rot if the Mistress hears! Mistress *Grindon*! Remember?" John Fytton's tone had turned from anger to sarcasm as he addressed his eldest son.

Jack Sharpe fled, and above, Jordon of Bolyn stood, white with rage. Jack deserved his head kicked in! But the other two! He'd not put himself in jeopardy to gain revenge, but he would bide his time. One day, when they were least expecting it, he would see them suffer.

Had Jordon but known it, his father was at that moment having similar thoughts about Sir John Grindon. Oh, aye. If circumstances had been different that night he'd have made an end of the man with his bare hands, and probably have been hanged for it! As it was, William Hesketh had likely saved Geoffrey Bernulf's life. He stamped his feet impatiently in the January frost. Isabel must be having trouble slipping away. The Fyttons had been in residence at the Hall since the new year revels, by and large, making the most of Grindon being away. They still felt an affinity to the place, even though they had failed in their bid to bring Isabel de Orreby to wed with Thomas, Grindon seeming a gentleman compared to the rough, uncompromising soldier. Still, she'd learnt that lesson. And how sweetly he had enjoyed the woman who had once been his virgin conquest on the banks of the Bolyn. When the call had come for her to attend the Court and Queen Isabella, Geoffrey had once more felt that he was no more than peasant to the Mistress. But Isabel was not a weak woman. She had insisted that she must go. John was her husband. If she did not obey him, he would not rest until he had discovered the cause, and the last thing she wanted was Mister Grindon returning to Gawsworth. He was better, she had persuaded Bernulf, kept happy amongst his courtier friends. Geoffrey sighed. At least he knew her body would be unmolested. And Jordon had remained at home. But now she was back and had sent Petronilla with a message asking him to wait for her at the stable tonight. The night was black. There could be snow by the morrow. Inside the stable the tunnel door creaked briefly. He went inside.

"What is it?" She was less than a shadow and he more felt than saw her.

"Geoffrey. Geoffrey." Isabel moved towards the sound, feeling up with her hands for his face before entwining her arms round his neck.

He smelt her warm femininity. Felt her softness. Became roused by her obvious need for him. He kissed her with a tenderness he hadn't experienced with any other female, enjoying the closeness of the firm shape pressed against him, knowing he held in his arms the Mistress of Gawsworth Hall. And one day . . . He smiled to himself as he led her towards the pile of hay. He'd been worried.

Thought there was something wrong. But it seemed that she was lonely, and he was only too willing to oblige her.

Isabel drew on the strength that was Geoffrey Bernulf. Trembled under the assertive touch of his exploring hands. A man's hands. Hard and possessive. Yet experienced and thrilling. Broad, muscled shoulders and swelling biceps bore witness to archer and thatcher, as much as the sinewy calves, sheep-skin wrapped and leather thonged, pronounced him peasant and tiller of her soil. But his greatest skill was surely that of lover. Never in the history of the world had a man made a woman feel so complete. Never in her life could Isabel de Orreby love another man so much. She only wished that this was the sole reason for escaping the supervision of the family her mother had married into. She wished more than anything that she didn't have to tell him his son had been recalled to Court by order of the King. London was a den of thieves, and the Court more devious than a nest of snakes.

3

THE Grand Banquets of October 1313 were occasions of pomp and ceremony intended to show the people of England that the internal strife was over and that the King and his Earls were once more clear in their joint direction. North. Against the Bruce. And as Edward, beaming with satisfaction, took in the sight of the greatest men in the land together with vast numbers of their respective households, feasting and making merry, he felt he had made a new beginning. All his problems were over and in the future he would be as revered as his father had been. As his musicians played in the gallery, acrobats performed their tricks and jugglers demonstrated their skills. And the cooks brought in course after course of meats and pies and puddings. An ox had been roasted slowly for three whole days, the cavernous interior, relieved of the guts and offal, being stuffed with plover and partridge, capon, thrush and pigeon which stewed to perfection in the juices. The tastiest of these were presented to the Queen. And the Queen was once more with child.

"Jordon." Edward beckoned the youth to him before whispering secretively in his ear. Jordon smiled and nodded vigorously, then turned and left the Great Hall.

"My Lord?" Queen Isabella raised a questioning eyebrow. "Who is that boy? He seems to be at your elbow by the minute." After the early years of her marriage it was difficult not to be suspicious of every sycophant. Especially handsome, ambitious young men.

"He is squire to one of my knights. Sir John Grindon. You have allowed his wife Isabel to serve amongst your ladies."

"Ah. Isabel. Yes. So the boy is from . . . ?" Isabella waited.

"His name is Jordon of Bolyn, the Bolyn being a river running through the estates of John Grindon. And by the normal way of things he should still be in Cheshire doing tillage and learning to thatch. His father is a thatcher, and an archer in my service from time to time. A good man ... What was his name? Ah it escapes me, but I well remember the promise I made him. The boy is good with figures and stood out like a sore thumb amongst the others, and as his only wish is to be a great merchant ... " King Edward shrugged, smiling at his young Queen.

"I see." Isabella studied her husband carefully. What manner of man had she really married? Had he not been King of England he might have been considered inventive, playful, kind, and generous to a fault. As it was, men thought him gullible, weakwilled and easy prey. Whoever heard of Kings making promises to peasants and actually remembering them? Edward was impossible! And as for Sir John, with his polished manner and immaculate grooming! Isabella wouldn't trust him as far as she could throw him!

Grindon was pleased with himself, having managed to get himself seated in the company of the Earl of Gloucester and his brothers-in-law, showing himself well and truly ensconced in the King's party. Lancaster and his allies smiled and nodded over their cups at the proceedings, determined that the Ordinances would be carried out to the letter. Tonight they supped together, but John Grindon, along with many other knights present, wondered how long the truce between the King and his cousin would last. He listened to the conversation around him.

"So we'll be on the march again come spring."

"Aye. But to my mind it's been too long since we showed them that we exterminate vermin! My guess is that we'll muster at Berwick. The Bruce might have winkled his way back into Dundee and Edinburgh . . ."

"Not to mention Perth and Roxburgh . . ."

"As you say," Gilbert, Earl of Gloucester agreed, washing his greasy fingers in a silver bowl of rose-water. "But Mowbray had decided on the battlefield . . ." He paused thoughtfully. "Stirling! Not the first time we have clashed beneath those walls." Gilbert poured honey and cream over a dumpling crammed with dried plums. "But it is the first time a site was chosen a twelve-month in advance."

And that, the knights acknowledged,

would make it quite a battle! It would not be a year for forays, skirmishes and retreats. Sir Philip Mowbray had made certain of that. Stirling might be made of stern stuff but the man had been forced to make terms or surrender immediately and the agreement was that unless the English army could relieve the stricken garrison by midsummer of the following year the Scots would take Stirling without a fight. And such an outcome was unthinkable!

Grindon thought briefly of his enlarged holdings since his marriage. How many men would he be required to bring to the King's army? How many archers? Infantry? Retainers? At least he had no worries about their skill and courage. He'd fought with them before and would lose no sleep on that score. Rough they might be. Able, they most definitely were! He'd struck a fine bargain when he married Isabel de Orreby, despite the problems it had caused him. Love, to him, had always been the ethereal, misty memories of his mother. Vague and beautiful. Merging in his mind with the holy purity of the Virgin Mary, Mother of God. Melting and blending into a single entity. Isabel, pure and naked on her wedding night, had seemed the physical embodiment of the sanctity of Woman. He could never tarnish that divine image.

At that moment Grindon noticed Jordon return to the Hall carrying a flat box. Nimbly the boy made his way through the throng of servants waiting on the tables, avoiding the crouching forms of hounds and other dogs as they scavenged amongst filthy grasses and strewings on the floor. Underfoot was a mire of bones and slops and ordure which could only get worse before the night was over. But this was the accepted thing. The knight watched the slim lithe figure. So young and vital. Long curls, blacker than night, and eyes to match. Eyes filled with the eager sparkle of hope, occasionally deep and brooding, but always bright with intelligence. His skin was still soft as a girl's, though lately the chin had shown a hint of shadow . . . John Grindon swallowed painfully as his throat constricted with emotion. Such love was always bitter-sweet. How wonderful to help the man escape the boy. And yet how sad to leave innocence behind.

Hugh de Spenser had been toying with the remnants of a mellow pear, listening as Gloucester put forward future plans and strategies and wondering whether the King's plans would coincide. Edward wanted confrontation. With a resounding victory he would defeat not only the Scots, but his opponents on this side of the border too. England would be behind him to a man. De Spenser was about to put this to the courtier beside him when he noticed that Grindon's interest lay elsewhere. The man was almost choked with tears. Pushing back the lock of straight fair hair which habitually fell across his brow, Hugh followed his neighbour's dismal gaze thoughtfully. A young, dark-haired squire was bowing to the King as he handed him what looked like a jewel box, and, like Grindon, King Edward was giving his full attention to the boy. Not a muscle twitched in Hugh de Spenser's face. But his thoughts raced. King Edward might *play* the happy husband ... But the embalmed body of Piers Gaveston was still unburied ... And could a leopard ever change its spots?

As the King fastened the golden torque, set with a large ruby, around his Queen's neck, the glimmer of an idea crystallised into a positive plan in de Spenser's mind. Gaveston had been too vain. Too churlish. Too stupid. But what could a man with brains achieve in similar circumstances? There was no sense in letting the King's eye remain on a rustic squire when an elegant and charming courtier could advise him in everything he needed to be advised in ...

And his lip curled in a sardonic smile as John Grindon left the board, dashing away a tear as he went to relieve himself behind the screen.

* * *

"By God, lads, there's prospects ahead!" Sufficient quantities of ale had put William Hesketh in optimistic mood. He'd been disgruntled when John Grindon, after travelling with him, chose to ignore him once they were at Court. He glanced across at the group surrounding the Earl of Gloucester. But perhaps it was as well. They were a stuffy lot who only laughed at their own jokes. Better to sit on top of your own midden than be buried under someone else's!

"Prospects there'd better be!" The menace in Robert Lewer's tone was somewhat undermined by the large belch which followed.

The company Hesketh kept at the banquet was over-indulgent, under-cautious, and determined to prosper. By hook or by crook! Companions of circumstances, not one would turn his back on another in peacetime. Yet in battle they owed their lives to the fierce, almost insane loyalty of their fellow men-at-arms.

"What of the Master of Odiham?" Will Ogle spoke the words softly, leaning towards Lewer. "An accident, was it?"

"Aye. It was." Robert Lewer narrowed his eyes, daring Ogle to argue. They'd both sell their grandmothers for tuppence.

"Not much of a loss to the world." Hesketh poured oil on troubled waters.

This was neither the time nor the place to let the ale talk.

"I'd have had that castle of his but for de Spenser. It's my guess he'll be kissing the King's arse before long. Fornicating bastards, the lot of them. But my memory is long . . ."

"You'd be a fool to stick your neck out." Ogle stared at Lewer, eyeball to eyeball. "You're already banished from the King's household and have the cheek to sit there eating his food!"

"And will you point that out to the stewards?" Lewer's hand was on the hilt of his dagger as he leaned forward.

"Either drink up or shut up," Hesketh murmured quietly, kicking the hard-faced man on the shin.

Lewer struggled with his temper through an alcoholic haze. There would be another time. And another place . . .

William Hesketh watched bleary-eyed as Robert Lewer slid slowly and silently from sight under the table. A wolfhound sniffed uncuriously at the prone figure. Then it cocked its leg and pissed, marking its territory before continuing its feast of discarded bones.

★ ★ ★

"Make way, you scum, make way. Jordon of Bolyn deigns to sup amongst us." Richard de Bettoyne made a great show of pushing Simon Barford and John de Gisors off the wooden bench, removing his cap to ostentatiously dust the seat with it. The younger element at the feast had spent the last few minutes making jokes at Jordon's expense whilst he was still out of earshot.

"Aye, I'll lower my standards just this once," Jordon grinned.

"So long as it's only your standards and not your gaskins!" Richard had to duck as Jordon aimed a playful blow.

"Jealous?" Jordon fluttered his long-lashed eyelids exaggeratedly, glancing coyly but cautiously at the King as he did so. With an effeminate gesture he slid onto the seat beside his friends and lifted his cup in a mischievous salute.

Simon, who had just filled his mouth, almost choked with laughter, spitting half-chewed food across the table. The other two laughed till they cried.

"Would you . . . I mean, do you?"

Richard wiped his streaming eyes, nodding to where Sir John Grindon peered morosely into his cup. The others controlled themselves, waiting for the answer. Jordon was good company. Easy to make a friend of. But . . . ! It was well known that he was Sir John's squire, and of late, Sir John had been less than discreet about his feelings for the boy.

"Do I?" Jordon paused to finish his drink. "Do I what? Take advantage of situations? Make the most of what the Good Lord gave me? Aye. I do. And so would you if your life had started as mine did."

"And how was that?" John de Gisors, like de Bettoyne and Barford, descended from well-connected stock.

"Not so well as it might have done." Jordon thought fleetingly of the tiny cot beside the river where first his grandmother, Sybil Bernulf, and then Christiana, his father's mistress, had looked after his worldly needs. So far as they were able. He had grown up with his father's dreams. How many times had he heard how the estates of East Cheshire had been stolen from Old Bernulf by the

Normans? How many times had his father sworn to regain Gawsworth Hall for his son? But if the father was prepared to live off dreams, the son was not.

"I've been to Gawsworth. 'Tis a fine Hall." Simon remembered the night he had first encountered Jordon. The lad had been in a vile temper at the thought of being left behind by Sir John.

"And should be mine, if everyone had their own." Jordon spoke softly, fingering the silver ring Sir John had given him at Yule. "But," he shrugged off the thought, "it isn't. And never like to be. So I look to other goals."

"And don't care how you achieve them?" Richard asked.

Jordon leaned forward over the table. "My father has a dream and I have seem him grow old on it, not having the courage to make it come true. Why wait for the apple to fall? Why not reach up and pick it from the branch? One day I shall be rich. Not only that. I shall be respected."

John de Gisors sniggered. "Respected? We saw you pout at the King. Mayhap Piers Gaveston began that way and I'd not say he was *respected*."

"Mayhap Piers Gaveston sought enemies more than friends." Jordon smiled amiably. "I seek friends, and accept friendship in whatever guise it comes. Are we not friends?" He looked at the three in turn. "Yet have you ever been uneasy in my company?" He paused. "No. Nor should you be."

Through the ale's joviality, the others acknowledged the fact. He'd never shown the slightest inclination of anything untoward with them. He could drink them under the table. Use a sword as well as any. Talk of politics and religion. Even eye a passing wench . . .

"Have you ever thought . . . " Jordon wondered whether they could stomach a little philosophy . . . "That the times we live in are shaped by the people we share those times with? The things others do can alter our direction; our wealth; our comfort."

"Oh, aye." Simon Barford looked across at the group surrounding the Earl of Gloucester. "They scheme and plot for their own ends and we get dragged along . . . "

"So they do." Jordon followed his envious glance. "And in doing so, take sides, hoping that their leader in his victory will share the spoils. Choose the wrong side and they're dead! And those?" He nodded to the rougher end where Robert Lewer had just dropped to the floor like a boulder in a landslide.

"Real men. Fighting men." Richard de Bettoyne could not help admiring the way Hesketh and Ogle survived. They appeared to live life to the full. Everything to excess. Always noisy. Always in the middle of any action.

"And always changing sides," Jordon observed. "Always looking over their shoulders, wondering if another has an advantage he himself has overlooked. Never content. Not loyal. To their masters or themselves. They'd slit your throat as soon as look, and that after sharing your bread the night before. Whichever side they choose, they'll end up losing."

"So what's the answer?" Richard asked. "Gaveston came undone by his methods. Lancaster may yet do the same by his. The Earls are no better, the knights fight amongst themselves . . . "

"Look to yourself. That's the answer. Use them, but do not depend on them. Consider your actions carefully and do whatever must be done . . . "

"Do whatever must be done . . . !" John de Gisors' mouth dropped open. "So you have . . . ! You do . . . !"

Jordon laughed loudly. "Don't look so shocked! Sir John has been a great help. And now the King takes an interest in my well-being. And this gains me entrance to other doors. There are those in this world who think to use my contacts with King Edward to gain themselves advantage. And so I let them believe. But at the same time I use their skills and knowledge."

"To what ends?" Richard marvelled at Jordon's attitude. So matter-of-fact. So uncompromisingly prosaic.

"Wealth. First I intend to make a personal fortune, dependent not on the bounty of others, but on trade. I buy. And I sell. So long as I sell dearer than I buy, I cannot lose."

The faces of his three friends were a picture. Had they heard right? Was

Jordon of Bolyn saying he was a *merchant*?

Jordon nodded. "And if you take my advice you'll look for ways to make your own fortunes and not wait for a pat on the head or a kick up the arse from the likes of them!" His glance encompassed most of the men in the Hall. "But if you want play . . . " He winked.

"Play?" Simon felt justified in being wary. He would be sick at the thought of being used so by Hesketh!

"Meet me on the Chepe, tomorrow. After noon." Jordon's tone steeped the invitation in mystery.

"The Chepe?" Richard raised an eyebrow.

"Aye. All the foreigners of the world and every merchant in the Port of London passes through Chepeside. But I do more than just business there . . . "

"Foreigners . . . ?" Simon was still uncertain.

Jordon chuckled. "I do have certain arrangements made at the George . . . "

The following day, curiosity overcoming trepidation, the three friends met outside the George Inn and were welcomed in by Meg. Jordon stood on the hearth, grinning. And beside him, to their enormous relief, stood a girl. Girl? She was scarce more than a child. Angareta Boundle with her huge innocent grey eyes, had them gaping. They didn't know quite what they expected of Jordon, but this wasn't it. A girl, yes. But so young. Too young! Too naive for the games they had come to indulge in.

"Meet Angareta, slave to her mother, in whose house I lodge, from six till noon. And slave to my desires from noon till dusk. Do you love me, Angel?" Jordon smiled down at her. The girl melted under his gaze. She didn't need to speak.

"As I told you last night, we should make the most of the things the Good Lord provides. So if you'd care to toss dice, or draw straws, to decide the order, I shall take Angareta to a room above and carefully explain that *my* friends must be *her* friends . . . " He laughed as John de Gisors licked his lips and Richard de Bettoyne wiped his sweaty palms on his shirt. Simon Barford sat down suddenly, his face pale.

There were more sides to Jordon of Bolyn than there were phases of the moon. And none of them malicious.

The Cheshire hedgerows were bright with lush new grasses and speckled with delicate spring blooms. Crops were sprouting on the tillage and lambs shook their tails with the joy of being alive. So why, Christiana wondered, did happiness elude her? Then she sighed softly. Did she still have to ask herself that question? After all these years? The woman's lips met in a thin, hard line, revealing her inner torment. Of course she was right to question. Isabel was a married woman. Why wasn't she with her husband at the Court of the King? Why were they always apart? Wasn't the woman happy with one man? Did she have to keep a man like Geoffrey Bernulf hanging on her apron strings when she could have so different a life? It wasn't fair! If only . . . Christiana dug her nails into the palms of her hands in frustration. If only she dared slip Mistress Grindon a potion!

She'd tried it once, many years ago, and made the situation a thousand times worse. Isabel's brother had somehow drunk the brew instead, though how the error had occurred was a mystery. Richard de Orreby's death had left Isabel heiress to Gawsworth. And that had been all Geoffrey had needed. If Sir John Grindon got so much as a hint of scandal, Bernulf would be a dead man. If the Fyttons, still thinking they were Lords of all they surveyed, ever suspected what was going on under their noses, he'd be slaughtered in minutes. Yet still Isabel encouraged him . . .

Still lost in thought, Christiana limped slowly on to the path leading to the shepherd's cottage not far from the edge of Three Mile Wood. Petronilla's herbs were growing well. And the sow had a fine litter. And the shepherd's daughter, Benedicta, was becoming a pretty young woman. It all looked so neat and sweet. Why? Why did some have everything, and others almost nothing at all? Why had God seen fit to make her barren?

"Good morrow, Benedicta."

The girl didn't speak but bobbed a curtsey in response. Her eyes remained lowered and her bottom lip protruded sulkily. With a squeak, the cottage door opened. "Christiana. I thought I heard you." Petronilla stood aside to let her visitor enter.

"What is the matter with Benedicta? She isn't ill?" Christiana stood in the centre of the one-roomed home. The fire blazed and the hearth was swept, and a dish of curds stood ready for refreshment.

"In love." Petronilla bustled about getting cups and small ale.

"In love? At her age?" Christiana was startled.

"'Tis all in the child's mind. A case of absence making the heart grow fonder. She's been pining over Jordon ever since the night she and her father found the lad strung up from a tree stark naked. But from all I hear, he won't be venturing to these parts again. No more than his master . . ."

"Sir John? Not coming home?" Christiana was dismayed.

Why, Petronilla wondered, did her tongue work faster than her brain? "But of course, I don't believe a word of it!" She tried to rectify the mistake. "What man in his right mind would leave Gawsworth for long with the Fyttons hanging round like an evil stink?"

"Are they at the house now?" There was hope in Christiana's voice. Isabel would be hampered with her mother in residence to chaperone her and Geoffrey would be certain to return to the cot for his comforts.

"No." Petronilla wished she could say otherwise. "With the call to arms . . . they have things to attend to in Macclesfield. Our own men have enough to keep them busy in the same cause." She tried to laugh lightly. "Cursing and swearing at the youngsters for their clumsiness. Archers? Never! they declare. If victory depends on the young men of today then we are doomed!" She laughed again. "They were never young themselves. Never inexperienced. They've forgotten the weeks and months they spent at the butts just so they could win a pig at Barnaby Fair. Do you remember?"

"How could I forget?" Christiana looked at the other woman.

"That very day we plighted our troth on the banks of the Bolyn." Reaching down inside the neck of her gown she pulled out a leather thong on which hung a brown and brittle token.

"What is it?" Petronilla reached out to examine the object.

"A rush ring. He fashioned it there and then, saying that if I loved him I would not force him to wait until he had gold." There were no tears in Christiana's eyes. She had done all her weeping. But she still hoped.

"The man's a fool and I always said so," Petronilla declared. "Or are women the fools for putting up with them?" she shrugged. "'Tis like the world. Six o' one and half a dozen o' t'other."

"It isn't *her* he wants." Christiana had convinced herself on that point. "It's that stupid dream of being Lord of the Manor of Gawsworth. They say old Bernulf still haunts the stableyard where his cot stood in ancient times and I swear that so long as Geoffrey Bernulf breathes it is true. While he curses the loss of his estates daily the old man has no hope of resting easy in his grave. Wherever that may be."

"Aye." But the response was hesitant.

Petronilla felt sorry for the crippled woman. Christiana deluded herself. It was so obvious from the look in Geoffrey's eyes. It was no longer the idea he was in love with. It was the Mistress Isabel. Nor was it the youthful lust of yesteryear. There was now a deep understanding between the two. Never revealed by word or public deed. But it could be felt in the air surrounding them. Vibrant and powerful. Mistress and peasant they might be, but they were woman and man first and foremost.

"But here." The shepherd's wife changed the subject. "I have the slugs, collected by the light of the full moon as you instructed. And here are the thorns."

"And warts," Christiana murmured, "are easier to mend than hearts." Smiling ruefully she took a length of rush from her basket, together with a small linen bag and a thin leather thong. These she placed on the floor beside the pot of slugs and sprigs of hawthorn.

"Give me your hand."

Petronilla held out her right hand. Two large warts sat on her knuckles, rough and yellowing and ugly. Muttering under her breath, Christiana slowly rubbed the growths with separate leaves, her eyes closed and her body swaying slightly from side to side. The other woman shivered, glad that it was daylight outside and that her daughter was nearby. Magic frightened her.

After several minutes the leaves were removed and thrown onto the fire. Christiana watched carefully as they curled in the heat before turning brown and bursting into flame. She nodded, satisfied. "Now," she said, turning back to Petronilla. "Place your hand flat on the board."

Petronilla obeyed, watching as her friend selected the two largest slugs from the pot. These were placed on the warts and tied firmly around with the rush to keep them in place. Occasionally they writhed a little, trying to escape their confinement, but apart from that there was no sensation. It was the strange incantations which sent the shivers down Petronilla's spine, and the sight of Christiana in communion with another world.

"There!" The witch-woman opened

her eyes. "The evil is removed and all we have to do now is let it destroy itself." So saying she released the slugs and impaled each one on a thorn before slipping them into the tiny linen bag and tying it around Petronilla's neck. "As the slugs die and rot, so will the warts." There was something sinister in her smile. "If only Isabel Grindon could be removed so easily!"

Petronilla laughed nervously, never sure how far the witch-woman was prepared to go. "Does Geoffrey not come home at night? Who cooks for him? Washes for him? Shares his bed? I'd be more worried about the Scots than the Mistress these days! 'Tis only next week our men begin the march north most probably. Berwick next June, so Ralph said this morning. God keep them!"

Christiana half smiled at that. "Geoffrey will be safe." The seven charms sewn inside his clothing would ensure it. And the special oil with which she would anoint him as he slept. Magic was a mighty weapon.

★ ★ ★

"Lift that arm! Shoulders level!" Geoffrey Bernulf growled at the youngster. "Who ever heard of a hunch-back archer! Straighten up, lad! Use your muscle!" He moved on to the next. "That's better. Now, hold it there. Here! You!" He called to the imcompetent he had just left. "Watch Francis here. See how he stands. The shoulders. Now *you* do it." He watched another feeble effort before shaking his head and moving on. Picking up his own bow he fitted an arrow. Some were born to it, he thought. And Francis Miller, Dickon's younger brother, was one of those. Carelessly he lifted his own weapon shoulder high and, standing feet apart, twisted to the target and loosed the shaft. The young men watched, awe-struck. No wonder he was considered to be the best. No wonder they called him Bernulf the Archer. And one day *they* would shoot like that, they all promised themselves. If they lived long enough.

"Good shot. That wins the pig in the poke, I should think." Ralph Dane slapped his friend on the back.

"Aye. All I ever win is the pig in the poke!" Geoffrey grinned ruefully, glancing up at the Hall.

"Liar." Ralph guessed more than he knew, but then again, he was a good guesser. "Do you think *they'll* win through?" He nodded towards the youngsters at the butts. "Stirling is never an easy battle as my cousin Banaster will testify. He was nearly parted from his soul there some fifteen years ago if the tales he tells are true. Even at Falkirk . . . " He fell silent, remembering.

"Aye. Falkirk." Geoffrey thought back to that day. Their first real battle. And Jordon Marton. Christiana's brother. Would he ever forget the sight of the lad, his fair hair matted with his own blood, fighting so desperately for his life? And losing. "It was Gurney . . . Remember Gurney? who showed me how to kill that day. Jordon. The friend I named my son for . . . Aye. We were not much different from these lads here, and we survived. Most of us. They'll only see the need to kill when they see the enemies' eyes. They'll be fine when the time comes."

"What goes on with Thomas Fytton?" Ralph asked thoughtfully. "He's normally never away from these parts when there's war to talk of."

"How should the likes of us know that?" Geoffrey was bitter against anyone with a right to live at the Hall, however tenuous. They say the problems with the Earls are over, but I wouldn't put Friday's fish on it. Not if Fytton and Robert Holland are anything to go by. Thick as thieves, those two. And all for Lancaster. If it ever comes to it, they'll be against the King, mark my words."

"There's a lot think that way," Ralph murmured.

"Not you?" Geoffrey sounded disbelieving.

"No. Not me. But it's as well to have a care who you talk to these days. Adam Banaster, for example. He's all friendly and charming . . . Especially to my wife . . . But!" Ralph left it there.

"He's always paid his dues to Lancaster so it's natural, I suppose."

"Aye. But think of Falkirk. Who did he fight beside? Us! And whose banner were we under? John Fytton's, for Mistress Isabel who was at that time unmarried," Ralph explained.

"And now, Mistress Isabel is married to Grindon." The name almost stuck in Bernulf's throat.

"Most definitely the King's man. So we are for the King. But after all the trouble, who are the Fyttons for? As you say, Thomas sticks to Holland. Lancaster's man. What of his brothers? John and Hugh? And Banaster is not for Edward, I know for certain," Ralph Dane the shepherd narrowed his eyes as he spoke. "And there may be others we counted as friends on the battlefield who have changed their allegiance. We may have more enemies than the Scots to deal with."

"True. In my case, very true." Geoffrey spoke quietly, almost to himself. "But it is I who seek revenge. Not him."

"Ho! Mister Bernulf. There's a message from the Mistress!" The two seasoned archers were interrupted by Jack Sharpe as he came flying down the grassy bank at the edge of the butts.

"Another message, eh?" Ralph nudged Geoffrey with a wink.

"A message to say that there's a message. From abroad." Jack came to a halt breathlessly.

"From where abroad?" Geoffrey asked, not really expecting an answer.

"From Sir John, I think." Jack scratched at his head in excitement and shuffled from one foot to the other. "For when Tilda gave the man meat I heard him say he'd come from London and was on his way to Carlisle with more messages. And Sir John is in London . . ." He smiled broadly, pleased with himself at remembering so much.

"Can you keep this lot on their toes?" Geoffrey asked Ralph.

"Anything for a friend," Ralph grinned, scratching at his crotch suggestively. "I'll get Tom Helesby out of the line to help. He won't be rushing off to his old woman yet awhile. She might be near forty years but she's a lustful bitch from what I hear and if he's home afore dusk he's half dead by dark."

But Geoffrey Bernulf was already on his way leaving Jack Sharpe to loiter at the edge of the practice ground, sucking his thumb.

The great Hall seemed empty but he glanced round cautiously before making his way to the stair leading to Isabel's room. Better to be safe than sorry. But Jack had not followed him and Tilda must be about her business in the kitchens. And Petronilla, so Christiana had mentioned this morning, was being treated for her warts. And all the Fyttons were over at their house in Macclesfield. Plotting. Somewhere above him a door opened.

"Geoffrey," Isabel whispered.

"It's very quiet. Not a soul about. What's this about a message?" He closed the door behind him.

Isabel paced the floor, unable to relax. She had known it would happen soon but even so had hoped for another day. Or two. "He's coming. Tomorrow."

"Grindon?" Geoffrey clenched his fists. His heart missed a beat and then began again, twice as fast.

"For roll-call and muster. Then he will lead his contingent north . . . " There were tears in the emerald eyes as she looked at him. "I don't want you to go . . ."

"Hey, Goose." He folded her in his arms as she ran to him. "Would you have me branded a coward? You've seen me go before and never wept."

"But then it was different. We didn't know each other . . . "

"Oh, no? Have you forgotten the hut in Three Mile Wood? The evening on the banks of the Bolyn? Didn't know each other!" He kissed the tears away. "We knew each other more than most, even then."

"Not like this . . . Not like it's been since . . . "

"Since we discovered your husband's predilections." He couldn't keep the harsh note of hate out of his voice. "And that is one good reason for going."

"What?" Isabel looked up into his dark eyes, trying to read his meaning. Her palms were pressed to his chest and she could feel the hard, taut muscle. He smelt entirely male; of horse and earth and sweat. His jaw was firm; his hair an untidy tangle. He was a man. Her legs trembled. Her knees weakened. She clung to him.

Geoffrey Bernulf saw the lower lip begin to shake. He kissed it. Then, as the tears began in earnest, he kissed her harder, lifting her from her feet and laying her calmly on the bed.

"He comes tomorrow? Then we have today."

"Don't! Don't say it like that. It sounds so final." Isabel didn't even try to control her emotions. Desperately, hungrily, she watched as he slowly undressed, wanting him to hurry, yet wishing time could stand still. Her eyes and mind missed nothing. It was as if she needed to imprint the memory for ever in her head. The sun-bronzed skin. The muscled shoulders. Slim waist. Narrow hips. And legs which could walk the length of England in a month without faltering.

She felt his warmth. His strength. He was in command, as he always would be.

"I love you. I love you." She couldn't tell him enough. "Don't ever forget."

"I won't." His voice was husky as he gazed down at her through heavy-lidded eyes. "And when next I come to you like this, you will be a widow. I swear it."

Then he took her, as though it were his right.

4

THEY had left Berwick on the seventeenth day of June, nearly twenty thousand men in all and more than two thousand of them cavalry, marching confidently north through Lauderdale towards Edinburgh. Robert Bruce with his vastly inferior numbers wouldn't stand a chance. On the way they had seen ample evidence of the destruction wrought by Bruce on what had been English holdings, and Edinburgh was no exception. The windswept castle, high on its towering ridge, had been devastated. All that remained of the clustered buildings was St. Maragaret's Chapel, the tiny church commemorating one of England's saintly daughters who had by circumstances been forced to flee north. How the poor woman had come to find herself married to King Malcolm of Scotland was open to debate.

"What now?" Will Hesketh heard a rumble from men camped on the other side of a craggy knoll. That was always the trouble with Edinburgh. There didn't seem to be a flat piece of land for an army to set down, and certainly not an army this size. It was impossible to see what was going on around the corner, or down the dip, or beyond the gully.

"Maybe the women have arrived." Robert Lewer tested a piece of harness he'd been having trouble with. There were usually two or three hundred women following the army, for one reason or another, but there were never enough to go round. "Here, lad, put this with the rest of my tackle." The fetch-and-carry boy scurried to do his bidding then stopped dead.

"It's the King," the youngster managed to stutter. He'd never expected to see the leader of this great army so close. What should he do? Kneel? Cheer? He didn't know so he just stood there, mesmerised. Those with more presence of mind bowed their heads.

"Hale and hearty men? Rest easy, for tomorrow we have a hard march ahead and I should like us to reach Falkirk before dusk, God willing."

The Earls of Gloucester and Hereford, accompanying the King, nodded agreement, for once. Hugh de Spenser, sitting his horse with a certain casual arrogance behind the Earls, smiled mirthlessly, his lip curling with a hint of insolence. Then the small party turned their mounts and continued to make their way through bands of men round flickering campfires.

"Bastard!" Lewer spat into the flames as he sat down to eat.

"Who? The King?" His companion bit into the stale pasty he'd been carrying since Berwick. There was a maggot in the meat and he picked it out, squashing it between finger and thumb before continuing to eat.

"De Spenser," came the snarled reply.

"Still resentful over Odiham. Forget it. There are other places better." Will Hesketh thought of Totleworth and the delightfully rich Elbora.

"Aye. And most of them going *his* way. What did he get . . . Berwick? Only Moray's land! And promises of others as we come to them. And if you ask me, there's more to these gifts than meets the eye." Robert kicked at the burning wood with his heel of his boot to stir the fire into greater flame. "A lot more."

"Oh, aye?" Hesketh studied the other man for a moment. Were his words only wishful thinking? Or had he heard something?

"I've been watching. And I'd stake the wife's life on it."

"You're not married," his squire spoke up cheekily.

"All right. My whore's life then, if we're to be accurate. De Spenser was in the thick of it when they set up the Ordinances, and used his position to advantage. He was with the Earls as fast as any. But then, when all this came about he put himself on the King's right hand. And he gets closer by the minute. Especially since Queen Isabella lost the child she carried. My information is that Edward has scarce been near his wife since she thrust his second son too soon into the world."

"Hugh de Spenser is too shrewd to fall into the same trap as Gaveston. He's like his father. Crafty . . . " Hesketh broke off speaking as he heard his name called.

"Ho! Will Hesketh! You thieving whoreson. Whose property do you have your eye on this time?"

"Not guilty," Hesketh called back to Thomas Gurney. "And at least I'm on my arse. Not creeping through the dusk like some."

"Touché," Tom replied, scarcely pausing his step. "But I'm off in search of former comrades. Cheshire men. Archers. Have you seen them? Under Grindon's colours, I believe."

Robert Lewer dragged up a gobbit of phlegm from the very bottom of his lungs and spat forcefully. "And he's another I'd soon not turn my back on."

Will Hesketh showed his broken tooth in a broad grin. "You're becoming obsessed, Rob. Not a good thing in battle. I've ridden with Grindon and come to no harm though I admit that when it comes to currying favour he's the best . . . " He waved at Gurney. "Over toward Wells o'Wearie. At least, that's where they were heading when I last saw them."

★ ★ ★

It seemed to Geoffrey Bernulf that the twenty miles between Edinburgh and Falkirk stretched longer with every step, and every step brought back painful memories. The twenty-second day of June was hot, but after the rain of the previous days the road beneath the feet of the marching hordes was a quagmire. It had been hot the year they carried Jordon Marton home. By rights their friend should have been left with his dead comrades in Scotland, but at the age of eighteen they had viewed things differently. The only thing they could think of was to take him home where he belonged. What, he wondered, would Jordon think of the men they had become? Ralph hadn't changed. They'd known even then that Petronilla would have him to husband. Ralph was too easy-going to do anything about escaping from her clutches, despite the brief interlude with Margaret Cherry. It was not really surprising that Benedicta Dane and Alditha Cherry could have passed for sisters! Geoffrey glanced at Ralph as he plodded silently along beside him. They'd shared so much. Good times and bad. Yet their ambitions were so very different.

Geoffrey kicked a stone aside as he walked. Jordon might not have considered himself a friend of the thatcher these days, had he lived. Having lived with Christiana all these years without marrying her he would have had no right to expect her brother's friendship. They might even have ended up as enemies, though he doubted it. But then again, there had been a time when he actually admired John Grindon for his skill in battle, and been grateful to the man for his life. Yet today he planned to murder the filthy scum-bag. People changed with the times, he decided. As he himself had changed. He still had his original hopes of marrying Isabel and owning Gawsworth. Once it had seemed nothing more than a foolish fancy, whereas now, with Grindon proving to be less of a husband than Isabel had hoped for, and Gaveston's ruby still hidden in the tunnel at Gawsworth making him a rich man, there would be nothing standing in his way. Once this battle was over.

The route was familiar and despite the heat, Geoffrey felt his skin shiver with goose-flesh as the road swung past the ancient ruins of Rough Castle. He'd caught a couple of rabbits there and they'd shared them on the eve of battle. Jordon had been uneasy, but Banaster . . . Geoffrey glanced at Ralph, a question on his lips. Then he blinked in the bright sunlight. Jordon's fair hair shone like spun gold as he marched at Ralph Dane's shoulder, his face still youthful, still eighteen years old, and alive with excitement.

"Ralph!" Geoffrey stopped dead in his tracks, almost tripping the man behind him. Then he blinked again. There was no one there. Just the shepherd, his weathered features furrowed in a puzzled frown.

"Get on, Bernulf!" The familiar tones of Adam Banaster prised him from his strange waking dream. "You look as though you've seen a ghost. Not getting old are you? Frightened of a fight?"

Geoffrey gazed at Ralph's cousin blankly, his mind racing. He *had* seen him! He was certain. Old Mother Marton had, so it was thought, dabbled in things not spoken of. And her daughter

Christiana could work miracles with her potions and spells. Was it possible that Jordon too had powers they had not known of? He caught up with his friend, Adam Banaster following.

"You're shaking, comrade. I never thought I'd see the day when Bernulf the archer took fright." Adam's red hair was ablaze in the sun. Startling in its flamboyance, as was its owner.

"Can you never keep your stupid mouth shut?" Ralph rounded on Banaster. "And what brings you in with the Cheshire men anyway? I thought you were for Lancaster?"

"The Earls have sent contingents, in accordance with their obligations. And of course they only send the best," Adam told him cheerfully. Lancaster, Warwick, Surrey and Arundel had refused the King's summons on the pretext that according to the Ordinances Edward should have consulted the magnates before declaring war. Everyone knew it was just an excuse.

"Then Lancaster admits his own lack of skill by staying home with the women," Ralph couldn't help remarking scathingly.

"What does he hope for? An English defeat?"

"Oh, heaven preserve us from such an outcome!" Adam raised his eyes skywards. "With King Edward leading us?" The incredulity was too exaggerated to be sincere. "And Hugh de Spenser at his elbow? And those charming, selfless men, Gloucester and Hereford . . ."

There had been talk of nothing else for days. Something was causing bad blood between those two, though the men had little idea of what the trouble was. But then, there was always a certain amount of friction between individuals, even when they fought shoulder to shoulder. And sometimes the cause was far removed from present situations. Ralph marched solidly forward, determined to ignore the man he knew to be less than loyal to the King. A man who had for years been over-familiar with Petronilla, and but for that woman's sharp tongue and moral stamina might have seduced her from under her husband's nose. Adam Banaster irritated him. The chatter of the young archers, eager for first blood, irritated him. In fact, Ralph Dane was out of sorts with the whole world and for the life of him couldn't understand why.

They rested at Falkirk a mere six hours and then were on their feet again and making for Stirling along the old Roman road. Approaching the area known as Torwood with its scattered clumps of trees and rocky projections the leaders slowed the troops warily. Scouts had seen movement up ahead though further investigation disclosed nothing more than flattened earth and broken branches. King Robert had watched the approach and retreated to the more thickly wooded area of New Park, crossing the Bannock Burn and avoiding The Pows with its lattice of thin streams and muddy flats. The Scots dug furiously in the stretch between the Burn and the woods, creating pottes and covering the holes with branches, leaves and clods of grass. A horse with a broken leg would be little threat, and once Edward realised the trap he would order his men to the only way through. And that way would be well defended.

Bernulf sat on an outcrop of lichen-covered rock, fingering his bowstring. Testing it with a single experienced finger.

He watched as young Francis Miller checked his flights for the thousandth time and William Davenport chewed at his fingerends as though he hadn't eaten for a month. He knew how they felt. Terrified. Yet exhilarated. Wanting action. Yet lacking confidence.

"Don't worry lads. This is the worst part. The waiting."

Francis managed to smile. William continued to chew. "Ho, Ogle! What news?" Geoffrey hailed an old friend.

"An argument! The Earls are fighting over who dies first!" He made his way over to the Cheshire men. "Gloucester, as Constable, expected command of the vanguard. But Hereford, as Hereditary Constable of England, claims automatic right to be out in front."

"What a time to pick a fight." Even Adam Banaster could see no cause for merriment in the situation.

"But that isn't the only bone of contention. Mowbray had safe conduct from the castle and has just ridden in to say that as the King's army arrived on midsummer's day, honour is satisfied. We need not fight."

"What!" A dozen men were on their feet immediately. "Not fight?"

"They're not seriously contemplating a retreat?" Geoffrey couldn't believe his ears. After all this marching! Forty miles in two days, and the men's blood boiling for a fight at the end of it. Twenty thousand men! The Bruce could only have half as many at most. An English victory was assured, so if the Scots thought they could now turn round and all go home sweetly after dragging their enemies all this way, they would be forced to think again.

He was right. Mowbray's suggestion fell on deaf ears and the army advanced on New Park.

"Stand fast!" Sir John Grindon signalled his standard bearer to halt. The Cheshire men were behind the vanguard and, owing to a small rise in the land, looked over them to where the woods thickened. Emerging from the trees was a small band of horsemen, obviously Scottish, and obviously unaware of the huge body of men less than half a mile away.

Rumour rippled through the ranks like a wave creeping slowly up the shore.

"It's him."

"Him?"

"The Scottish King."

"It's the Bruce!"

Henry de Bohun, Hereford's nephew, was amongst the first to realise the possibilities and without thinking further, set his lance and charged. King Robert wheeled his horse to face the oncoming enemy, the thrill of conflict already in his veins, his senses all alert, ready to be triggered into action. He pressed the horse's flank; leaned forward as he dug in his heels. His fingers gripped more firmly round the strong shaft of his battle-axe.

De Bohun charged on. This was his moment. With a single blow he could win victory for England. He saw the Scot turn. He saw him kick and rein. Henry took aim, sweat scalding his eyes and the drum of hoofbeats in his ears. He missed.

Robert the Bruce swung the heavy axe upwards and round in a huge arc. On a lesser man the arm would have been wrenched from its socket. The curved blade fell. Sir Henry's helm split with a metallic crack before the skull disintegrated, spattering the horse with a mess of blood and brain.

The woods seemed to spew out jubilant Scots and in the skirmish which followed, the English vanguard was forced to withdraw towards Torwood. If King Edward was to make best use of his superior numbers, the Scots would have to be tempted out of the trees to engage in battle on more open ground, but it was dusk before the men heard what was afoot.

"Bernulf!" Sir John Grindon rode up to the rocky encampment of his archers, his eyes scanning the band of men. "Take the strongest. A dozen or so . . . Cross the Bannock Burn," he pointed down towards the meandering torrent, "and make your way over to the Pelstream Burn. Men from the garrison will meet you there, along with others from our army. And waste no time!" The knight pulled his horse around and galloped back to the King's tent.

It took the fittest, most muscled men of the King's army not much over two hours to produce make-shift bridges out of planks, boards, and even doors, provided by the men from Stirling Castle. Then the move began. Cavalry crossed first, many of them picking their way through the torrent without artificial aid. The infantry followed, swearing and cursing when they slipped, some in over their heads, some up to their knees, and all with wet feet. Bags and baggage, weapons and ammunition, tents and waggons. And the food and ale. All landed on the firmer ground between the two burns safely and it was the ale barrels which provided the solace after the duckings, to greater or larger extents, that the foot-soldiers had suffered.

"So this is where the Bruce will meet his end!" Tom Helesby looked around him with satisfaction, the ale warming his belly and boosting his morale.

"I wonder how? Which one of us will loose the shaft?" Young Francis had a gleam of hope in his eye.

"Or wield the sword, or thrust the dagger," his brother Dickon brought the lad down to earth. "Don't forget, son. When your quiver is empty, the battle won't be over. Not by a long way!"

Will Davenport's mouth dropped open

for a moment. Then he selected another finger and began to gnaw it to the bone.

"What think you of this move?" Geoffrey Bernulf spoke quietly to Ralph Dane, not wanting to be overheard.

"I'd have soon kept the archers to the higher ground. We'll be hard pressed to get best advantage here." Ralph prodded the earth with his dagger absentmindedly. "And though the ground is firm enough now . . ."

"Aye. I thought the same. There's little enough elbowroom between the streams, and if there are any trickles underground the weight of this army will soon bring them up." Geoffrey looked at his friend thoughtfully. "You've been quiet these last couple of days. Are you all right? Not ailing?"

"No. At least I don't think so. It's just that I keep remembering things. From the past. Things I haven't thought about for years."

"What kind of things?" Geoffrey picked a scab of dried mud from his knee. He'd felt the same. Ever since he'd seen that vision of Jordon Marton.

"Oh, I don't know. All kinds of things. Margaret Cherry . . . "

"Those kind of things!" Geoffrey grinned.

"Not just that." Ralph shook his head. "Barnaby Fair. The lambing pens. The lakes at the Hall. Ridge and Cloud and Three Mile Wood. Petronilla. Benedicta. Everything!" He looked bemused. "I've never been like you. I'm just an ordinary shepherd. Not much imagination. But ever since we came to Falkirk and beyond, my brain had been haunted by . . . I don't know what. Except to say that I cannot bear the sight of my cousin Banaster."

"Banaster!" It was Geoffrey's turn to look puzzled. "The man's a rogue, we all know that from the tales that go about. And many a woman has lived to regret his sweet-talk. But when he's come into Cheshire there's been no trouble."

"No. I know. Whenever he turns up you can be sure he's keeping away from the trouble he's caused elsewhere." Ralph shrugged with a self-conscious smile. "Perhaps I have more imagination than I give myself credit for."

Bernulf tried to laugh reassuringly. "'Tis a mixture of midsummer madness and eve-of-battle nerves. Come on! Let's drink to victory!"

The two men, friends since childhood, raised their cups and drained them.

* * *

Midsummer's eve had been all Christiana could have wished. Alone, on the summit of Shutlings Low, she had spent a night of vigil in air so crystal clear that she could see distant horizons as though they were within arm's reach. And for one instant, as the sun dipped for its brief rest below the edge of the earth, she saw the sparkle of water at the south-west tip of the world. In the time it took for the fire of Belenus to reappear on the other side of the mountains in bright new cloak of molten gold, the silent woman had criss-crossed the moorland height a hundred times, limping painfully on her crippled leg, collecting dew. This she poured into the ancient hollow of a boulder and, sprinkling it with vervain, made sure of Geoffrey Bernulf's safe return.

It was a five-mile walk back to her cottage by the River Bolyn, but Christiana was in no hurry now. She had done what she had to. The shortest night was safely over. But in the early morning, sound travels far and she shuddered as she heard the dog. Somewhere on the other side of the wood it howled long and hard. The witch-woman muttered a nullifying verse. She would not like to be the person outside whose door the hound bayed. It was the harbinger of death.

Inside her tiny home, Petronilla the shepherd's wife bustled about getting dressed and making the place neat before she left for her work at the Hall.

"Benedicta! Go out and throw something at that stupid hound. What's got into him this morning I can't imagine. Move, girl." She gave her daughter a push towards the door. "Now then." She spoke to herself when there was no one else available. "Have I done everything? The pot is on and sure to boil afore noon. The rabbit is hung. The hens are out." Though she'd probably have a devil of a time trying to get them in again at nightfall, away from foxes. With a last glance round the room she left, closing the door behind her.

"What was wrong with him?" she asked her daughter as the dog disappeared, its tail between its legs.

Benedicta shrugged her thin shoulders. "He soon gave up when I threw a stone. It hit him on the nose."

They made their way up towards Gawsworth Hall, past Daisy Meadow and over the wooden bridge across the lakes. It was going to be warm again. Like yesterday. The air was still and the only sound was that of a blackbird high in the oak beside the house. It was always quiet when the men were away.

"I . . . I wonder if Jordon will be all right." Benedicta could think of nothing else. "He hasn't fought the Scots before . . . "

"Of course he'll be all right." Petronilla was sharp. "They'll all be all right. Don't they always come home?" She pushed thoughts of Christiana's brother and Dickon Miller's brother and two young cousins from her mind. "The best archers in the world come from these parts. Why shouldn't they be all right?"

"Jordon isn't an archer." Benedicta's eyes were moist.

"No. But from all Mistress Grindon tells me, he can use a sword as well as the best of them. And you should stop all this mooning over what can never be yours. Mister Jordon moves in higher circles than the likes of us and will most likely be married to a lady of the Court in London one of these fine days. Apart from which, there are other things about Mister Jordon which do not have me thinking highly of that young man."

"What things?" Benedicta was on the defensive.

"Nothing you need bother about, seeing as he'll be seeking a wife elsewhere," her mother retorted.

"If you mean the horrid things Richard Fytton has been whispering, then it's all lies anyway. Richard Fytton is spiteful and I hate him."

"And you'd better watch your tongue, Mistress, for if Mistress Cecily hears you speak so of the apple of her eye you will be in for a rough time about your duties. Never bite the hand that feeds you, and most of our fare comes from the bounty of the Hall. If you can't speak good of the Fyttons, say nothing at all."

"But I know Richard lies!" Benedicta was determined to have the last word. "Because Alditha Cherry says . . ."

She was cut off short by a sharp blow from her mother's fingers which had her ears stinging. "And I don't want you mixing with the likes of Margaret Cherry's daughter! If I so much as catch you wandering in the direction of Lane Ends . . . !" Petronilla pinched the flesh at the top of her daughter's arm causing her to wince and squirm.

"But why?" Benedicta rubbed her arm resentfully.

"Never mind why. Just stay away." She stepped aside as Jack Sharpe chased a squealing piglet out of the kitchen door. "I think the best thing for you is hard work. It will take your mind from mischief, so first you may bring water and sand and scour every pot and platter in the house."

Tilda, already about her work for an hour or more, smiled to herself. Those two would never be all sweetness with one another. They were too much alike, both wanting the last word in any argument and neither able to hold their tongue for more than a minute at a time. "Good morrow, Petronilla." Her tone indicated that she knew it to be anything but good for the other woman. Her plump fingers continued their steady rhythm, plucking out the grey-white feathers of a goose, some of which went into the basket at her side but most going onto the floor, where they lay in soft heaps, still warm from the bird.

Petronilla didn't bother to answer. She had too much on her mind to be in the mood for Tilda's barbed comments today. In fact, she was more on edge than usual, what with such a short night, and the dog howling. And then her daughter keeping company with the Cherrys! Mistress Dane straightened her coif and gave herself a mental shake. If there was any news from the north, then the kitchen was not the place to hear it. Mistress Isabel was the one to pass the time of day with for that kind of information. And she went through to the main hall.

"But surely," Cecily Fytton was saying,

"you will not allow things to remain like this. When your husband returns from fighting you will accompany him to the King's Court, not stay here alone. It isn't proper!"

"I feel *that* is between Sir John and myself." Isabel was not going to let her mother intimidate her as she had in the past.

Cecily sniffed contemptuously. Sir John was a foreigner. Why couldn't the girl have followed her own sterling example and married a Fytton? Young women these days had little or no respect for their parents. Thomas might be somewhat rough around the edges. A soldier, often as coarse in the presence of females as he was on the battlefield. Forthright. And a woman always knew where she stood with a man like that! Whereas with Sir John . . .

"Indeed, it is between the two of you," Mistress Fytton agreed with her daughter. "But such behaviour from the Master and Mistress will only make for gossip in town and village. I dread to think what may be said about you in Macclesfield on bread days! You should be seen together. Or all sorts of rumours will start. And the first subject will be your lover!"

"My lover?" Isabel's hand automatically went to her throat. God! They'd hang him! What had been said? Who knew? If Sir John had found out, Geoffrey was a dead man.

"No woman, once she has tasted the delights of the marriage bed, should be left to her own devices for very long. It begs trouble." Cecily nodded sagely. "And every other married woman knows it. So! They will invent a lover for you. And should your husband hear of it he will be entitled to beat you within an inch of your life!"

Isabel breathed again. No one knew. Except Petronilla. Her eye sought her maid's as she went about, tidying the hall, removing yesterday's debris.

"Sir John is the last man I can imagine giving me a thrashing. For one thing, he would not be foolish enough to believe such tales of me." Isabel thought of the way her husband looked at her. Almost as though she were a goddess.

"Then you know very little of men!"

her mother retorted. "No man in the world, no matter how courteous and charming, can stomach the idea of being cuckolded, with the world and all its friends laughing at him behind his back. And the best way to prevent even the slightest rumour is to keep your own husband happy in your bed. Not remain at home when he goes to Court!"

"Ah, Mother." Isabel smiled sadly. "'Tis easy to see you have never been to Court yourself. It is a different life. Everyone must be of the fashion, and fashion changes by the minute." She paused, glanced across at Petronilla who still busied herself on the other side of the hearth. They'd grown up together, albeit one at the Hall and the other in a cottage, and there was nothing her maid didn't know about her early life. Mistakes and all. But since her marriage, the distance between them had widened. Petronilla still chattered nineteen to the dozen, but these days it was a one-way flow of information. Still, she must guess at the truth, what with Geoffrey returning nightly to Christiana, and the witch-woman being a friend of Mistress Dane.

Isabel remembered her lover's promise the night before he left, straight and proud, with the best archers in Cheshire at his shoulder.

"When next I come to you, you will be a widow."

Perhaps it would be as well if she prepared the ground with her mother. What harm in her knowing the truth about Sir John Grindon now?

"Fashions may change," Cecily sniffed at what she considered to be her daughter's short-sighted attitude. "But a wife is still a wife no matter what else comes and goes."

"And there is my dilemma." Isabel gave the older woman the benefit of a steady, knowledgeable gaze from her emerald-green eyes. "Sir John is not truly my husband. Not in matters of the flesh . . ."

Cecily's eyes widened. Then she looked disbelieving. "Not consummated? But Mistress! The wedding night . . . Ah . . ."

"Yes, Mother. Now you remember the wedding night. He sent everyone away early. Even Petronilla." The maid had stopped her show of activity and looked up as her name was mentioned.

"Then he didn't . . ." Cecily Fytton frowned. Then her face cleared as though she had suddenly understood something. "So it's true. The tales about that boy. Jordon of Bolyn. Richard and Hugh were right." She'd ignored her sons' innuendoes about the young squire, putting their jibes down to very understandable jealousy, the foundling being shown the life at Court whilst they, descendants of the great Sir Richard Fytton who had both the lordship of Fulshaw and the lordship of Bolyn, were overlooked and left to roam in idleness in Cheshire.

"Aye, Mother. It's true. Though Bernulf the thatcher, the boy's natural father, I believe, took Jordon in hand and showed him the error of his ways." Isabel tried to hide a smile. "But I'm afraid it would be impossible to mete out the same treatment to my husband."

"Not consummated . . ." Cecily murmured thoughtfully. There were possibilities here! And the moment her husband, John Fytton, and his brothers returned from Scotland they would be informed of the situation without delay. Grindon had snatched Gawsworth from under their noses. Or so it had seemed. But armed with this piece of information they had every chance of winning it back. Thomas was not yet married.

"I think that after noon we shall send for Nicholas Bailiff and Timothy Reeve." Cecily was decisive. "To make sure that all is in order with the estate and the accounts. We must not shirk our duties to our menfolk!"

Petronilla wiped her hands on her skirts, as was her habit, and returned to the kitchen. What was Cecily Fytton plotting now? The shepherd's wife grunted to herself. Whatever it was, if it concerned Mistress Isabel, they'd best get permission from Geoffrey Bernulf before they did anything at all.

★ ★ ★

It was in the dew-damp light of dawn that the first movement could be discerned on the edge of the wood, and as they emerged further the Scots were seen to have separated themselves into four divisions. King Robert was in charge of the rearguard.

"Making ready to run when his men fall," Adam Banaster observed.

"I doubt it," Geoffrey muttered, shaking his head. "He has the advantage for advance, but we . . . We could have trouble, with the Pelstream to one side and the Bannock to the other."

"Our cavalry will make short work of infantrymen, though who will ride to meet them is anyone's guess. A bet on it? Hereford or Gloucester?"

"What now?" Ralph Dane narrowed his eyes as he gazed across at the enemy. In a single movement, the whole of the Scottish army had fallen to its knees, reciting the Paternoster.

"There!" Banaster laughed. "They pray for mercy already."

Then the advance began, with Robert Bruce leading his men in a solid wall of spears towards the English.

"They should let us in first to thin them." Bernulf wasn't happy at being in reserve. "We have broken the schiltroms before and could do it so now. Then the cavalry could go. What is Edward doing?"

Unknown to most of the men on the field, the King was embroiled in a fierce argument with his brother-in-law the Earl of Gloucester.

"Let the archers loose as soon as they come into range," Gilbert de Clare suggested. "Scatter them before the cavalry charge."

"After all the fighting between yourself and Hereford I'd have thought you would be only too pleased to be the first out there wielding your sword. Or do your bowels now turn to water at the idea?" Edward had been scornful, only wishing it had been politic to ride out himself. But the risk was too great.

Gloucester turned on his monarch angrily. "Do you call me a coward?" His blood was up and he threw caution to the winds. Hauling on the reins he raised his sword in a signal to his men, and before anyone had realised what was happening the vanguard was charging, Gloucester at its head, riding like a madman toward the enemy to prove his courage. He was amongst the first to be slain.

As the English vanguard fell back the Scottish King sent Moray and Douglas into the fray in support of his brother, and for the first time King Edward saw that the battle was not going to be the foregone conclusion he had supposed. The unflinching line of spears marched ever nearer and combat was once more engaged, this time with Edward in the thick of it, his presence urging the English forces to ever more daring deeds of valour. But still the schiltroms held, the Scottish army unswerving in its remorseless determination.

"Holy Mother, why don't they use us?" Geoffrey Bernulf wiped the sweat from his palms on his jerkin. "The cavalry look to be doing as much harm to our men as they are to the Scottish turds. They *must* call us!" He looked around to make sure that the men would be ready when the word came. As it must. And soon.

"Move to the flank!" The strong voice of Thomas Fytton was heard above the clash of steel and screams of the injured. "Archers! Men of Cheshire!" He raised his arm to show the direction and wheeled his mount, his huge frame, clad in blue and silver, had all the air of authority needed.

"At last someone sees sense," Geoffrey breathed. "Make way behind Fytton."

"Ho! What goes?" Sir John Grindon, wrestling with his wounded horse, arrived.

"To the flank!" Thomas shouted at him. "Only the archers can break the schiltroms. They are flaying our cavalry!" He pointed to the bloody gash beneath the torn trappings of Grindon's mount. "Our men are the difference between victory and defeat! They are our only hope!"

"Pembroke gave no such order!" John Grindon's ire was up at the thought of the upstart Fytton taking his men without permission.

"And if we wait to ask him we shall have lost. God knows, you imbecilic whoreson, it may already be too late!" Thomas Fytton was not a man to mince his words at such a time. With a mighty roar he led the Cheshire archers forward and round, to a point where they were at an angle to the main body of the Scots. Grindon, unwilling to abandon the men from his estates to another, followed grudgingly. As they reached position, he turned, searching behind. To his relief he saw that Jordon of Bolyn had escaped the melee in the centre and was hard on his heels, his sword arm still intact.

From their new position the archers could see more clearly the English difficulty. They fought on too narrow a front, and as Bernulf had predicted, the underlying water had surfaced to hamper any manoeuvrability they might have had. In the middle of the main battle they could see the King, fighting like a demon, his skill putting his knights and Earls to shame. The June sun flashed time and time again on his weapon as he raised it and swung it at his adversaries. Then, to everyone's consternation, King Edward disappeared as though his horse had fallen under him. And had they been closer, they would have seen that this was indeed the case. The animal was dead. Speared through. Separated from his shield bearer and without a mount, it looked as though all would be lost right then. It was Hesketh, swearing oaths with every breath, who caught a riderless horse and lifted his

King into the saddle. A mighty cheer went up as William Hesketh, exposing his broken tooth in a crazy, laughing grimace, whirled his sword above his head before thrusting it through the throat of an unfortunate Scot.

"Positions!" Thomas Fytton's voice thundered out.

Sir John Grindon galloped past the massed archers to a spot slightly in front and to the side. There he could be seen by the men and would be automatically in command.

"Take aim!" He sneered as Thomas lost control of the unit.

"Fire!"

Arrows filled the sky, the sound of the shafts whistling through the air persuading many of the enemy to look upwards. And then wish they hadn't. For the first time, gaps appeared in the bristling ranks. But Robert Bruce had seen the English move. Before the men on foot realised what was happening he had sent in the few cavalry he had, putting them to better use than bogging them down in the centre of the field. The archers were forced to scatter, or be cut down where they stood. They would have no chance of another shot. No chance of reforming.

"Come away, cousin." Adam Banaster somehow appeared at Ralph Dane's shoulder. "The day is all but lost."

"Not yet, it isn't!" Ralph pulled out his short sword, ready to engage in hand-to-hand combat. "See! The King still fights. We are not done by a long way!" He ran lightly to where a Welshman under Pembroke's banner was getting the worst of it, and with a sharp thrust of his blade successfully gutted the Scottish boy, leaving him writhing in a pool of his own blood.

Thomas Fytton faced the oncoming charge with gritted teeth, his muscles flexed and his brow running sweat. He saw their leader turn aside to the left, engaging Grindon in a fierce clash, their sword edges sparking fire. With a roar, he slashed precisely at the weld of a helm, splitting it to expose a grizzled head. A single blow, and the skull cracked. Then Thomas turned to the next line. There would be no stopping him today!

Geoffrey Bernulf was about to admit

to discretion being the better part of valour by making good use of his legs when he saw Jordon, sword drawn, facing the cavalry charge. The lad would never stand a chance. He shouldn't have been there anyway. He wasn't an archer. What was he about? Geoffrey rushed forward and grabbed his son by the scruff of the neck and pulled him towards a small patch of scrub.

"No! Let me at them!" Jordon kicked and screamed at the archer. It was no use. He was no match for the older man's muscles or determination.

Sir John Grindon heard a scream. It penetrated his mind through the stink of fear surrounding any man face to face with death. Jordon! The boy was hurt! For a second he hesitated, and Sir Robert Keith needed no more encouragement. The heavy swing of the sword caught the Englishman a massive blow to the shoulder, unhorsing him. With a thud he hit the ground, looking up into the leering face of his enemy. Desperately he struggled to get to his feet, but his arm was useless and his armour cumbersome.

Bernulf moved by instinct. He didn't know he had drawn an arrow and fitted it to the string until he took aim to fire. It had been an automatic reflex. The arrow was within a fraction of being loosed at Sir Robert's heart. Then Geoffrey Bernulf slowly and calmly lowered the bow.

"Fire! Shoot him!" Jordon was shaking with frustration and fear. "Shoot! Shoot!"

It was too late. John Grindon's severed head lay oozing in the mud three feet away from his body. And the archer took hold of the hysterical boy and dragged him out of sight. The horsemen had completed their task and turned back to the woods and their King.

"Why?" It was all Jordon of Bolyn could ask. "Why? You could have saved him." He trembled from head to foot as though frozen to the marrow. He couldn't get the sight of the jerking death-throes from his mind. Sir John, dead. The man who had been so kind to him. The man who had first taken him to London where he was now on his way to making a fortune. The man who had ... He turned to his father. "Was it because ... because he loved me? Is that why you killed him?" He clenched his fists as though to strike out. "Because if so, you had better make up your mind to kill half the men at the King's Court." He screamed the words into his father's face. "It is a way of advancement. Are you a fool that you can't see it? It does not prevent a man from having a girl or two for pleasure." Then his jaw dropped open as his father slapped him. Hard.

"I care nothing for you. Not now, nor ever. And what I did I did not do to save you from his clutches. There are other things important to me. Not only you." Geoffrey shook the young man hard, almost lifting him from his feet. "I did it for your mother's sake. And if you dare speak one word of this to anyone you will destroy not only me, but her too."

"My mother?" Jordon blinked. "I have no mother. I was told so by my grandmother. A foundling, she said. My mother could have been any one of the blow-by-nights you left with child. Only this one presented you with the results!" His words were bitter.

"You were no foundling. Your mother suckled you and risked her reputation for your life. Your mother is the only woman I have ever loved. Your mother is Mistress Isabel. And you, Sir, on her wedding night, took her husband to your bed. That wretched man, still twitching there, humiliated her so completely that she nearly lost her mind." Geoffrey Bernulf slowly released his grip on Jordon's clothing as his son stared at him, scarcely breathing. "And now, your mother is a widow."

At that moment Pembroke was slowly fighting his way to the King's side where he still remained in the thick of it, determined that the day would not end in defeat. The Earl realised only too well that things were going badly and that if the King should be captured, Robert the Bruce would have every ace in the pack. Enlisting the help of Sir Giles D'Argentan, the King was prised from his adversaries' clutches and, surrounded by a band of five hundred knights, rode across the Bannock Burn to safety.

The day was lost and the land littered with the bodies of the fallen, and the Bannock Burn, its make-shift bridges long since demolished, was awash with those who had drowned as they tried to escape the slaughter. In the face of such destruction there seemed little point in hating his only son. Life was too brief to waste on such trivialities. So Geoffrey Bernulf turned south, his arm about the bemused lad's shoulders, and began the long march home.

What he didn't know that day was that he left behind the body of his childhood friend. Buffeted by the torrent, the lifeless form of Ralph Dane had become wedged between two boulders, face down, the dagger protruding from between his shoulderblades hidden under the foaming water. It was two days later when Alexander Bell found it and washed it clean in the burn, rubbing at the curved bone handle to decipher the letters whittled into its surface.

"A and B." He chuckled. This must be his lucky day. A dirk with his own initials!

He had never heard of Adam Banaster, nor ever would.

5

"I'M sorry." Geoffrey Bernulf stood awkwardly, half glancing through the small window to cover his embarrassment.

On a stool beside the cold hearth Petronilla cried silently, tears streaming down her cheeks unchecked, her hands grasping Isabel's as though her own life depended on it. Ralph wasn't coming back. Not ever.

"Did you see him? Were you with him?" She sounded so hopeless. So empty of everything that had gone into the make-up of Petronilla Dane. The sharpness. The dominance. The absolute conviction that she was right in everything. It had all evaporated with the news of her husband's death.

"No, I wasn't," Geoffrey had to admit. "We were on the flank of Bruce's army, trying to break the shiltroms with our fire when the Scottish King sent in his cavalry to scatter us. It was the last time I saw Ralph . . . " His mind went back to that moment. Seeing Jordon, sword in hand, awaiting the enemy. And then deliberately holding his fire as Sir Robert Keith unhorsed Grindon before severing his head from his body. He had been too hell-bent on his own mission to keep track of his friend in their moment of defeat. "By Christ's blood, it should never have happened!" The archer smashed his clenched fist into the wall, denting the surface with his knuckles. "If they'd let us at them sooner! If Lancaster hadn't sent the bare minimum of his men, and those lacking in experience!" He turned to face the two women. "And now the word is that he has been raising a force of arms considerably bigger and better trained than the milk-and-water sops he sent to Scotland. I fear the King has more to worry about than the Bruce!"

Petronilla choked on a sob. What did she care for the King? Or Lancaster? What did any of it matter any more? There was nothing in the world to live for now. Moaning softly to herself she rocked back and forth on the stool seeing nothing but years of emptiness stretching before her. The walls closed in on her. She couldn't breathe. She had to get out, into the air. Into the fields where he had worked for so much of his life. She had to see his sheep. To tell them. To feel close to him for one last time. Wrenching her hands away from those of her Mistress, Petronilla jerked herself to her feet and running to the door of the cottage struggled with the latch, trying to escape.

Isabel ran to her, putting her arms around her distraught maid and whispering words of comfort.

"No!" Petronilla cried. "Let me go! I have to go to the flock. He would want me to!"

"Leave her be," Geoffrey suggested. "Mayhap she needs to be alone for a while."

Isabel loosed her grip on her friend and shook her head sadly as the woman tore open the door and disappeared along the garden path, her skirts flying. Then she looked at Geoffrey. What would she have done if he had not returned? She didn't even want to think about it. He had come back to her, and that was enough. And, as he had promised, she was a widow.

"Come here." Geoffrey held out his arms to her. "Petronilla will not mind us taking advantage of the moment."

She went to him slowly. Wondering. His arms slipped round her waist comfortably, holding her firmly but gently. Strong and dependable. Silently Isabel sent up a prayer. She too would have died had he not come home. But what of her husband? How had *he* died?

His kiss sent a thrill through every fibre of her being, making her tremble. This man was all she had ever wanted in the whole world though it had taken a long, long time for her to realise it. And he? Had he killed for her? Did he really love her enough to despatch John Grindon into the next world early?

"I missed you." He murmured the words into her ear as he kissed her neck before sliding his lips softly across her shoulder and down onto her breast. "God, how I missed you." Lifting her from her feet he carried her to the sacks of hay and feather in the corner which had served Ralph and Petronilla as a bed and there claimed the reward expected by returning heroes since man first went to war.

It was some time later that Isabel, still drowsy with the warmth and contentment of his love, heard the barely controlled excitement in his voice as he spoke, almost to himself.

"And now nothing . . . *nothing* stands between me and my inheritance!"

That same evening Isabel stood beside the window-slit of her bed-chamber staring sightlessly out over the dimming landscape. The sky was flat and low with a heavy layer of cloud hiding the distant hilltops. It would rain before the hour was up. She felt sick and ill. On returning to the Hall earlier she had been summoned by her stepfather to attend him in the solar used by her mother when she stayed at Gawsworth. And together they had faced her, smiling, but with satisfaction rather than friendship.

"Allow me to sympathise with you on the untimely death of your husband." John Fytton's thin lips formed the words with precision.

Isabel bowed her head in acknowledgement. That wasn't the meat of the summons. It was merely the trimming.

"And though you yourself may not have yet given thought to the situation, you will I think agree, that a woman of your years and standing would be unwise to remain in the unmarried state."

"There is as yet no heir." Her mother made it quite clear that such a thing could not be tolerated and that it was entirely her daughter's own fault.

"Sir, I have scarce donned mourning and feel it unseemly to rush into the married state again before my dear husband is cold in his grave." She looked straight at her mother. "The town was agog when Mistress Miller went from the Requiem Mass to the Nuptial Mass within a week. And as Sir John Grindon's widow I do command a certain respect from my workers and the common people."

Cecily Fytton gaped. Did her daughter dare to speak to her elders and betters in that tone? "Then you should know better than to compare yourself with the common people. What the Millers do is their concern. But how can they respect a Mistress who lacks children through her own obstinacy?"

"You are right, Daughter." John Fytton spoke placatingly. "It would not do to appear in too much haste. But at the same time you are aware that it is best to get certain things settled in readiness for the future. It is best to know where your future lies, as it were. Then there can be no doubts about your . . . attitude, shall we say, towards hopeful, would-be suitors." The stern smile indicated that he thought there was no need for argument on this point and the left eyebrow, slightly raised, showed that he expected her answer to be in the affirmative.

"I . . . " Isabel began to speak and then stopped. Would-be suitors? She had thought no further than Geoffrey Bernulf. But if she was realistic, she knew her step-father to be right. There would be other suitors. From any of the Cheshire Manors where a man was yet unmarried, or had lost his wife to the grave. They were always looking to increase their holdings. And what could she say against such suits? For the moment she could plead grief, but that situation could not last for ever. And in that time there would have been plans laid by any number of families in the area.

"So." Cecily nodded. "You see the sense of it. The sooner it is known that you are betrothed, the better for everyone's piece of mind."

"Not yet!" Isabel raised her voice. "For the love of God, it is too soon." Her mind raced. What could she do? What *should* she do? She had foolishly thought that at the age of twenty-eight she would be mistress of her own destiny, forgetting that it was not only Geoffrey Bernulf who had ambition. She heard again the words which had hurt so much.

"Now *nothing* stands between me and my inheritance."

Outside her bed-chamber the rain began to fall in a solid sheet of water, drawing a murky veil over the view. Isabel could just make out the lakes at the bottom of the slope, their surfaces pitted by the downpour and suddenly emptied of duck and waterfowl.

Was every man the same? Did any of them see her? Or did they only see her possessions? The things she could bring to them in a marriage settlement? Even Geoffrey. He had promised that Sir John would not return from Scotland, but whether that was to rescue her from her unhappy state for her own sake, or whether it was the only way he could be sure of becoming the Lord of the Manor of Gawsworth, she no longer knew. She loved him. But did he love her? Despite the ecstasy of their union on the sacks in Petronilla's cottage that afternoon, Isabel wondered.

Water began to drip through the corner of the roof as it always did when the rain was heavy and she moved to place the wooden bucket underneath the spot. The patch above her glistened, a dark, rotting section slicked with liquid and foetid with mould. The Widow Grindon smiled to herself. It was time she called in the thatcher. Yet, if her mother's plans came to pass, there would be no need. The Fyttons had great ideas. A new Hall, lower down, near the lakes. Greater and grander than anything in the whole of Cheshire, to hear them talk. She shuddered. It would be a fate worse than death to find herself married to that crude arrogant soldier, Thomas Fytton. Yes. She would sooner be dead.

If only Geoffrey hadn't said that this afternoon! If only it didn't niggle at her like a dog with a bone! She would have run to him. She would have told him of the threat to their future, and he would have . . . What? Killed them all? Isabel gave a small laugh which sounded almost hysterical. How could he kill them all? She thought of Thomas. Geoffrey was strong. But he could be gentle. He could be hurt. Despite his bravado, he knew himself to be of peasant stock and backed down in the face of superior authority. John Grindon he had hated for the atrocities committed with Jordon. Hated him enough to overcome his inferiority. But Thomas had never known the meaning of inferiority. None of the Fyttons had. Thomas was nothing but a hard soldier, without sentiment or emotion. Many were the tales she had heard around the hearth of the bounty he had taken in the wars. Of the women he had raped and left for dead. He had laughed as he described the way they screamed. Or fought. That was how he liked a woman. Screaming! Fighting. So that he could conquer them and end the day victorious. When Thomas Fytton wanted something, he took it and had no hesitation at despatching anyone who stood in his way. To him, death was a part of life. Geoffrey Bernulf wouldn't stand a chance. And the fight, she recognised, would not be over her, but over the beautiful estates in the north-east corner of Cheshire known as the Manor of Gawsworth.

★ ★ ★

It was hard to accept the fact that another year was almost half-way through. That another summer was just around the corner. Petronilla bent over the herbs, pulling chick-weed and buttercups from between the sturdy plants. Borage, balm, chamomile and fennel rubbed shoulders with lovage, mint and rosemary. The world carried on as though nothing were different. As though Ralph were still about to come home from the pens any moment, smelling of sheep and sweat and wanting his supper. The woman sighed. He had been a good husband. She wished she hadn't been so hard on him. There were so many times she could have held her tongue instead of scolding him for every little thing he did or didn't do. Oh, he'd only laughed. He'd known all along that she didn't mean one half of it. But all the same . . . She wished she could tell him. She wished she had just once told him that she loved him and that she forgave him his one mistake in tumbling Margaret Cherry. He'd probably only gone to her for a bit of peace and quiet when all was said and done.

"If only I could do it all again . . . "

"Is there anything more lovely than the sight of a buxom woman in communion with nature at sunset?"

Petronilla turned at the sound of the familiar voice. "Oh, Adam. I wasn't expecting you. I thought . . . "

"I know. And I was in London, on the King's business." Adam Banaster grinned cheerfully. "But things have brought me north again sooner than I had hoped to be. And I couldn't lose an opportunity of seeing the most handsome woman in

Cheshire, could I? Are you quite well?" He held out his hand to her, all solicitude and sympathy. "Are you able to manage, alone?" He led her gently towards the cottage. "I worry for you. Cousin Ralph would never forgive me if I did not take an interest in his adored Petronilla."

The woman's eyes filled with unaccustomed tears at these kind words. "I wonder you bother, after all the names I have called you in the past. The way I used to shout and insult you. Even lashed out at you with my ladle a time of two."

"Mistress, those times are forgotten. I think it might even have been the spark of fire in your anger which made me love you . . . " He watched as she tended the supper.

She stopped stirring the cauldron, with its hambones and bubbling peas. Making the pea-dollop had become a habit she could not break. "Love me?" Her eyes rounded in amazement. "Did I hear you right?"

"Aye Mistress. You heard. I love you, and have for many a year." He saw the slight tremor of her hand. The definite paling of her face. She looked startled at the idea. But not unhappy. There were events taking place in the world outside which would never come to the ears of Petronilla Dane and for almost a year he had been calling with condolences, keeping her warm for the moment when he could make sure of her loyalty to him. If he needed a bolt-hole, this would do very well, he thought.

The strangest thing happened to Petronilla. A faint, fiery tingle swept down her spine, and her legs lost their strength. She hadn't felt like this since she was a girl. Since the very first time Ralph Dane had accidently touched her arm after they had both attended hallmote, he having been fined for allowing his father's sheep onto the stubble before it had been depastured by the plough-animals, and she having paid heriot on her father's death. That feeling had been the signal to Petronilla that the boy was her future mate. And now it had happened again. For the second time in her life. She sat down on the stool by the hearth with an astounded thud as her knees gave way.

"Mistress." Adam fell on one knee

before her, a practised expression of concern on his face. His flowing mane of tangerine-coloured hair seemed to light the gloom of the cottage, removing the sadness of the previous months. "May I call on you for reasons other than duty to my poor, unfortunate cousin?"

The shepherd's widow struggled with this inexplicable change in her feelings towards a man she had always considered to be a braggart and a rogue. He had boasted of his holdings in Lancashire and of how his mother, sister to Ralph's father, had married out of the peasantry and into a line with far higher social prospects. Petronilla's main objection had been that most of their dealings were at best illegal, and at worst downright criminal. In fact, most of his visits to his Cheshire cousins had arisen through the need to make himself scarce. But now she looked at him as though for the first time. His clothes, though not new, were of the finest of wools, and his jerkin was not of the same somewhat rancid sheep-skin as her husband's. It was of dark green velvet. A little dusty, but velvet none the less. And she had to admit that although his reputation went before him, he had never harmed her nor said a wrong word. It had been she who had been the scold and the nag every time he showed his face. Just as she had been with Ralph. Perhaps it was time to make peace with her fellow man.

"I have no objection to your friendship, Sir." She smiled shyly.

"Then you make me the happiest man on earth." Adam Banaster took her hand and raised it to his lips as though she were the greatest lady in the land. But then, to be sure of her he lifted her gently to her feet and kissed her properly until the woman sighed and trembled in his arms. She offered no resistance. It was but a pace or two to the bed-sacks and before the Widow Dane could change her mind her late husband's cousin had brought her the only comfort, passionate and physical, which could assuage her grief.

From the open doorway Benedicta watched the threshing limbs and listened to the breathless groans in silence. Sobbing, she ran all the way to Lane Ends knowing that the whole world played the same game except her! It broke her heart to think of Jordon with Alditha, but she couldn't help herself. Waiting for him daily to secretly follow him home, she hoped and prayed that one day it would be different.

★ ★ ★

The setting sun poured molten gold across ancient mossy warts and bunions of the hillside; last remaining relics of a stronghold built in antiquity by Elelfleda, warrior daughter of King Alfred. Tom Helesby, leaning against the bole of an oak, lifted the cup to his lips. "A good hunt, but this suits me better!"

The whole hunting party had gathered, as was previously arranged, in a large glade on rising ground known as the Chamber of the Forest. "You're too idle to be a rich man," Geoffrey Bernulf grinned. It was well known that Tom had married Dickon's mother, a widow with a portion, rather than a penniless girl.

"And you're craftier than a fox!" came the rejoiner. "Leading the hunt away from your usual grounds."

"They don't mind." Geoffrey nodded to where their masters sat and discussed the rights and wrongs of the world. "The Fyttons will be feasting on meat for weeks." Deer and boar lay tied and bled beside the horses.

"And to us, the offal." Tom belched cheerfully. He had neither the patience nor the skill of his fellow archer when it came to laying traps and snares. Nor did he relish the idea of swinging from the gibbet at the corner of Gallows Field.

"I've work for you, if you want it," Bernulf put the idea to Tom, though he'd have put money on the answer.

"No. You'll not have me poaching . . ." Tom was quick with the reply.

"I'll do it!"

It was young Francis Miller who spoke. His elder brother looked up from the arrow he was repairing. "Oh, will you, now? And I'd have you remember that I am your guardian," Dickon interrupted.

"Hold on!" Geoffrey stopped them. "'Tis building work I meant. John Fytton had mentioned that he is continuing with plans he had before Sir John arrived on the estate."

"A new Hall?" Dickon whistled softly. "Once they have a foot in any door they are almost impossible to dislodge." He looked at Geoffrey quizzically. There couldn't be a common man in the area who hadn't heard of 'Bernulf's Dream'. They'd chuckled over the idea for years. As if he could ever hope to win the Gawsworth land from the likes of the Fyttons!

"Maybe. Maybe not." Geoffrey completed the restringing of his bow and laid it down. "Fytton or no Fytton, a new Hall would be the right thing."

"Then I can learn to be a builder," Francis said. "'Tis all right for you, Dickon. You have the mill, and a wife, and five daughters. Our father left me nothing, and unless I can learn to make my own way I shall never be able to take a wife."

"Listen to him! Fifteen years old and wanting an encumbrance!" Dickon pushed his brother playfully. "But . . . if Bernulf will have you . . . "

Geoffrey tried not to look too pleased. Francis was a good lad, and amongst the younger ones, one of the best archers. He liked him. Francis Miller was the sort of boy he had envisaged for a son. He glanced across to where Jordon sat with the Fyttons. On the edge of the group, but with them. Certainly not with the peasants on this side of the clearing.

"I'll teach you all I know, as my father taught me," he said, trying to keep the bitterness from his voice and avoiding the sight of his own son. He didn't for a moment recognise the ambitions and desires of his offspring that he had never been at pains to hide in his own nature. It was only the methods of achieving elevation which were different. "And," he added, "show you something I have long had thoughts of. New ways of building. New ideas . . . "

Francis couldn't have been more delighted. Francis the Builder. He liked the sound of that!

Jordon of Bolyn sat beside Richard and Hugh Fytton as they ate the food left for them, listening in part to the conversation of their father John and their uncles, Thomas and Hugh. He hated the young men more than he could ever tell, but not by so much as a flicker of his eyelid would anyone ever know. All he knew was that one day he would have his chance. He wouldn't rest until he had paid them back for hanging him naked from the tree in Three Mile Wood. And it would be so easy to have revenge one day. Because one day they would know the truth. He had more right to live at the Hall than ever they had. One day he would be able to tell the world that his mother was none other than Mistress Isabel, widow of Sir John Grindon, friend of His Majesty King Edward, second of that name. He hugged the secret to him. One day soon, when his mother was out of her long mourning and took his natural father to husband. Then he would be the legitimate heir!

"I enjoyed that!" Thomas Fytton belched loudly. "It makes a change to be able to hunt a quarry you can look forward to eating."

"It made a change riding to Wales instead of Scotland," his brother chuckled. They had recently returned from quelling a revolt.

"All the same, you can see Llewellyn Bren's point. Payne of Turberville should have had more sense. Fancy expecting to replace *all* Gloucester's officials overnight without a rebellion! Especially trying to replace a Welshman with so much power!" Thomas belched again, more comfortably this time.

"There was enough slaughter at Caerphilly to have started a rebellion throughout the whole of Wales," Hugh commented. "And it was as well the Bruce released Hereford from his captivity in time for him to lead against the uprising."

"And it didn't take us long to subdue them." John Fytton picked his teeth. He enjoyed a fight as much as any man, but by and large he preferred to be on his own ground. As Lord of Bolyn, he liked to keep an eye on what went on in the County of Chester. There were rivals enough nearer home, and it was as well to be aware of them. Others had forgotten this to their cost!

"The Welshman had courage. You have to agree." John Fytton looked at his eldest son. "What would you have done, Richard?"

Richard considered the question for

a moment. "Fought to the death, I should think," he grinned. "I can never imagine the idea of surrendering crossing my mind in the middle of a fight."

"Not even to obtain mercy for your followers?"

"Followers," he laughed, "are expected to follow, and I dare say had I been leading the revolt we'd have all ended up dead!"

"Which is perhaps why you are not yet a leader," his Uncle Thomas remarked. "Apart from the fact that it was your first taste of blood. But you enjoyed it?"

"Aye. And I'd willingly ride to crush another revolt tomorrow, should one arise."

"Ho, there!"

The call coming from along the main path into the clearing caught everyone's attention. Heads on both sides of the glade turned at the sound, recognising the advance of horsemen through the forest. In seconds, Robert Holland and William Hesketh had appeared and dismounted, leaving their animals with their squires and joining the Fyttons where they rested in the sequined sunlight amongst the tussocks of soft grass.

"Lancaster's men," Geoffrey muttered under his breath. "What trouble is there now? We're no sooner back from Wales than something else is afoot."

"It may be just a visit," Dickon speculated.

"Not by Holland's face. He's itching for something, and I'd say a fight if he comes to enlist Thomas Fytton. The two are hand in glove when it comes to plotting and murder. In the name of justice, of course. Should anyone else try the same tricks they'd be hanged without trial as felons."

"You think Lancaster still has designs on the Crown?" Tom Helesby kept his voice low.

"Think! How can you doubt it?" Geoffrey whispered. "He sent scarce a man against the Scots. Yet in his own parts he had men to spare. And . . ." He looked round to make sure they weren't overheard. "In all the raids we've heard of in the north . . . Led by Douglas and Moray . . ." he lowered his voice even further. "Thomas Lancaster's holding always seem to be spared! The Bruce has men as far south as Furness . . . And Lancaster makes not one move to repulse them. At this rate they'll be in Cheshire before we know it and the whole of England fallen to the barbarians."

"Not all the men of Lancashire are loyal to the Earl," Dickon couldn't help mentioning. He winked at Geoffrey with a grin.

"Ah. Petronilla . . . " Geoffrey didn't return the display of lewd humour. "There's more to that than meets the eye, mark my words. When the likes of Banaster stands up for the King against his master, all is not what it seems. I know him of old and he has ever been devious . . . " He stopped speaking as Dickon nudged his elbow. Jordon had moved nonchalantly away from the edge of the group of men and had sidled over towards his father. Jerking his head in the direction of a small copse he indicated that Geoffrey should follow.

Without attracting attention the archer made away from the clearing until both he and Jordon were out of sight and earshot of the others.

"Well?" He waited as his son turned

something over in his mind, looking for the right words.

"There has been some kind of revolt," he began. "In Lancashire. One of Lancashire's vassals has stirred a hornet's nest and the Earl has let it be known that he wants no such uprising brought to the King's attention." Jordon fell silent as he went over the information he had overheard. He thought of Alditha. And Benedicta. Both girls had that enchanting hair ... though Benedicta was too innocent to be of real interest, despite her love-sick glances. He well knew the rumour about the shepherd.

"So Holland comes for Thomas Fytton," his father nodded. It was as he suspected. Trouble!

"Aye. But that isn't all. Did they but know it they are in almost the right place. And Hesketh ... " Jordon hesitated. Could the man have been mistaken?

"What about Hesketh?" Geoffrey couldn't see what the delay was about.

"At the Battle of Bannock Burn, he was the one to lift the King onto a new mount when his horse was killed under him, and so stayed near His Majesty for the rest of the battle. And then, when the time came for them to lead the King to safety across the Burn of Dunbar, there were nearly five hundred knights in the party. When the King left Dunbar to sail to Berwick, most of his followers made their way by land. As did we." The boy looked at his father. Geoffrey Bernulf might not be a knight, but he had saved his son's life that day.

"And?" Geoffrey couldn't see where this was leading.

"And," Jordon continued, "it was then that Hesketh saw Adam Banaster in the gathering. He knew him as one of Lancaster's men, yet he was with the King when, unlike some of them, he had no need to put on such show of loyalty. And then Hesketh remembered something he had seen as they struggled to aid the King to escape. He has just told Thomas that he could swear he saw Banaster thrusting a dagger between the shoulder blades of a man.

"It *was* a *battle*," his father reminded him.

"Not just any man. Not a Scot. But a Cheshire archer. One who seemed familiar. Wearing a sheep-skin."

The final words fell into a silence, like the last raindrop into a puddle.

Geoffrey stood quite still. Banaster? Murdered Ralph? Surely not just to bed Petronilla? The man had bedded more women than Ralph had shorn sheep! And Petronilla, God bless her, was no beauty.

"The bastard! The base-born turd!" Geoffrey spun to face Jordon. "He has been stirring up trouble, you say? For his own ends . . . He'd see advantage in it, but there would be danger if he stood against the Earl. He would need a place to go to ground . . ." Geoffrey's fingers felt for the dagger at his belt.

Jordon noticed. He put his hand on his father's arm. "Best let *them* have him. *They* are above the law in matters such as these."

"I'd rot in hell first!" The archer was impatient to be away and back to the cottage by the wood.

"No!" Jordon stood his ground. "They'd swing you at the crossroads if you deprived them. It has to be this way!"

Geoffrey tried to shake off the hand,

but it held fast. "Thomas Fytton would be the wrong one to fall foul of. With Sir John dead, the Fyttons will take it upon themselves to extract the full price for one of Mistress Isabel's villeins." There was slight emphasis as he spoke his mother's name. A certain pride. Geoffrey Bernulf capitulated. He must be growing old, he thought. Or his son was really growing up at last. He knew the boy to be right.

"See to it."

Without another word, Jordon of Bolyn went back to the clearing where it took no time at all for him to disclose the whereabouts of one Adam Banaster of Lancashire. The man with the green velvet jerkin, and the tangerine-coloured hair.

* * *

Geoffrey Bernulf ran almost all the way back to Gawsworth Hall. The rest would have seen to the kill before they could leave the forest and no doubt Holland and Fytton would take some little time to decide exactly what they were going to do about the situation, and when. With luck, he would be the first there. And he could only pray that there would be the opportunity to speak to Isabel alone.

Edging cautiously to the door of the great hall, he paused. Voices, in gentle, muted harmony gossiped idly as the women went about their tasks. Petronilla had cleared the hearth and was preparing the kindling for a fire. Isabel sat on her highbacked wooden chair with its heartsease motif carved in proud relief. Her head was bent over her embroidery, the light from the window falling onto the rich glow of her chestnut hair as she concentrated her effort on the intricate work. There was no one else present. The two women were relaxed, and by Isabel's informal attire, were not expecting visitors, nor even the menfolk back for some time yet. Geoffrey cleared his throat to attract their attention. Both looked up, startled.

"There hasn't been an accident?" Isabel was on her feet, clutching at the linen she had been working on. It was her first thought. Jordon. Killed by a stag.

"No. No accident," Geoffrey was quick

to reassure her. He remained silent then, glancing briefly at Petronilla. Isabel understood that he wanted to speak to her alone. Something was wrong. Her heart began to beat twice its normal pace. If not Jordon, what? Petronilla didn't wait to be asked to leave and picked up the empty kindling basket and scurried out to the kitchen, giving Geoffrey a conspiratorial wink as she passed him.

"Then what is it?" Isabel waited as he approached, watching his face. There was no trace of humour or pleasure in his dark features. His black brows seemed blacker. The furrows on his face suddenly deeper. He looked angry. But there was more than anger in him. There was pain. Grief. As though an old wound had been re-opened and found to be septic.

Unmindful of being seen, he grasped her hand so tightly that her fingers were in danger of being crushed. "Banaster!" He spoke the name as though it was a curse.

Isabel's eyes rounded in surprise and she looked at the now closed door through which Petronilla had just vanished. "He is at the cot. Petronilla was telling me . . ."

"Petronilla has been taken for a fool. And so have we, over the years. How often has that man arrived out of nowhere and been given bed and board by Ralph out of some misplaced sense of family loyalty? How many times has he managed to be at our shoulders when battle was about to commence, despite the fact that he should have been under another banner and is not even an archer?"

Isabel listened to the tirade with her mouth open, unable to get a word in had she wanted to.

"That he was a turncoat, we guessed. So are many. That he was a rogue, we knew. That he appeared when his escapades took him within an inch of his life, we accepted without question. But this!" He broke off, too angry to go on.

"But what?" Isabel was still perplexed, but was beginning to understand that Petronilla was in an unhappy position with regard to her new love. "What has the man done?"

"Even the Devil will slight him for his

deeds!" Geoffrey smashed his hand into the wall, grazing his knuckles, ignoring the pain. "What he has done, Mistress is to take treachery as far as treachery will go. Having shit his hole full on his own patch, he comes to fill another's. Having first made sure that his cousin is in no state to return . . . "

"Are you saying that Adam Banaster killed his own cousin?" Isabel found it hard to believe after the glowing picture her maid had painted of the flamboyant, yet likable, suitor.

"And probably not the only man he's killed who thought him to be on the same side." Geoffrey looked straight into Isabel's eyes. "Petronilla will be in need of comfort." He turned away abruptly before she could question him further. "Be sure to keep her here today. On no account must she be allowed to return to the cot alone. Nor Benedicta," he added as an afterthought.

Isabel's hand went to her heart, as if to steady it. "Who . . . "

"He has been a fool as well as a murderer," Geoffrey laughed, without humour. "He deserves such an end as they will give him." Seeing her worried look, he explained. "He has turned against his master, Lancaster, and apparently started a revolt in the north to champion the King's cause. All very well if he meant it. But as usual with him, it was a cover for his own misdeeds. And Robert Holland means to defend the Earl's rights and privileges to the hilt! He may be on the wrong side, but Holland never wavers! He'll see rough justice done!"

"Holland?" Isabel saw the implications. "So Thomas Fytton is with him." It was a statement, not a question. The two were almost inseperable. The sight of Thomas Fytton gave her nightmares.

Geoffrey strode towards the door. "Don't forget. Keep her here." Then he left. He wanted to make sure that Fytton and Holland completed the job properly. If they failed, there would be others who were certain not to.

★ ★ ★

It was Jack Sharpe who spoiled the plan. He'd been fishing for part of the afternoon down at the other end of the lake, keeping out of Tilda's way and hoping at the same time to bring her to better temper with fish for supper. But he'd become bored. Nothing interested him for long. And the sun was hot. So he'd wandered into the shade of Three Mile Wood. Perhaps he might happen across a snare . . . But he hadn't. And before he knew it he was across Daisy Meadow, lost in a daydream, and pretending the summer-ripe grasses were Alditha Cherry's tresses spread across his bed-sack.

He blinked. He wasn't imagining it. It was Alditha. There. He could see her honeyed hair glinting in the shafts of sunlight as they turned the north copse into a strange and glorious place. A place to wonder at. A magic place. There she was again. Bobbing about in the lacy web of foliage, playing games with goblins. A smile of joyous anticipation lit Jack's normally blank features and he turned his feet in the direction of the flitting figure. It wasn't until he stepped from the full glare of the light into partial shade that he realised his mistake. It wasn't Alditha at all. It was Benedicta. And at the moment of his realisation, she noticed him and stopped the dance she was doing round the ring of toadstools in the tiny glade beneath the birches.

"Jack?" She smiled at him, still holding up her skirts with both hands, exposing her legs almost to the knee.

"I thought . . . thought . . ." he stammered. He was disappointed. It should have been Alditha. He could have tumbled Alditha and made her wriggle and squeal under him. He liked it when she squealed. And he was ready for it. His lance pointed skyward, just waiting to pierce soft flesh. Jack shivered. He moved forward. Slowly. Stealthily. Like a cat to a mouse. Perhaps Benedicta would squeal for him . . .

Her feet were dusty, and the spaces between her toes were black. But her legs, from ankle to knee, were the colour of cream. The brown stuff of her dress hid most of the girl's shape, but Jack could see that across the chest it was pulled tight, as though something inside was bursting to escape. And he knew what that something was!

"Jack?" This time the word was spoken with more trepidation. Why was he looking at her like that? There was a dribble of saliva hanging from the corner of his slack lips and his grimy fingers jiggled in a peculiar dance, itching to be at work. What did he want? Benedicta felt the first flutterings of panic in her stomach as her skirt fell back into place. She wanted to run, but her legs had somehow turned to stone. She wanted to shout, but her throat had suddenly closed, choking on nothing. He moved nearer without seeming to lift his feet from the ground. Like a snake. Slithering. Then his hand was on her, pulling at the neck of her brown woollen gown. The other thrust itself forcefully between her legs, the fingers probing violently through the hindrance of her skirts. And Benedicta at last found her voice.

How Jordon of Bolyn had managed to keep up with Rob Holland and Thomas Fytton he never knew. They rode like madmen through the forest, once they had made up their minds. The Earl of Lancaster would be the first to show gratitude if the uprising in his northern estates could be crushed before it had gained momentum, and they were already well committed to his cause. Jordon smiled grimly to himself as he spat out the dust sent up by their horses' flying hooves. With Sir John gone, there were those in Cheshire who would have to watch their words in front of their masters and their one-time friends. It was all too easy these days to fall foul of treason. And who, at this stage, could see who would be the eventual victor? Thomas of Lancaster? Or King Edward? As the young man ducked to avoid a low branch, he knew he had pledged his own allegiance years before. When he had first served his King with ale at the board at Gawsworth. Edward had noticed him. Him! Jordon of Bolyn! The motherless child of a peasant archer! He'd follow the King to the ends of the earth for the favour he had shown him then. It had been the door through which he had been able to escape and the start of his ambition to become the greatest merchant London had ever seen.

In the lane, beside the cottage gate, he pulled his horse to a halt. Fytton and

Holland had already disappeared inside, their mounts now idly grazing beside the hedge. From the open door, voices, loud and angry, betrayed the fact that Adam Banaster was indeed in residence in the humble cot and Jordon was on his way towards them when he heard another voice. A high pitched scream. Sharp with terror. It stopped. And then started again. He turned. The sound came from across the lane and down towards North Copse. He squinted against the sunlight, trying to see who was in trouble. Or simply fooling around. As girls did at times. But no! That was no game. The girl was frightened for her life by the sound of it. He looked again at the open door, wanting to be a part of what was to follow. And then again across at the copse. The screams were now continuous, which at least showed her to be still alive, though for how much longer, he wouldn't like to guess. Chivalry got the better of him and Jordon made for the trees up the slight incline above the cottage.

"Jordon! Jordon!" Benedicta had seen him running towards her.

The name, bellowed in his ear, brought all Jack Sharpe's survival instincts to the fore. Jordon. Of Bolyn? Here? It put an end to his futile thrusting before he had got half way to achieving his objective. Who would have thought the girl could find enough strength to keep him out? She didn't look much, but there was more muscle in her thighs than he had supposed. Snatching his smock down over his red-hot weapon and cursing under his breath, the frustrated kitchen-lad scuttled away into the undergrowth where he cowered, an animal gone to ground until the predator lost interest.

"Benedicta?" Jordon stopped three feet away from the girl. "I thought you were being murdered, by the noise. What trick is it this time?" Had the girl made all the fuss just to have him come to her? Had she seen him arrive and decided to make a game of it? If so he would slap her until she really cried.

"Trick? 'Tis no trick." And with a sob the girl flung herself onto her saviour, clinging to him as though she would never let him go. "It was . . . Jack Sharpe. He tried to . . . to . . ." Benedicta gave up trying to explain and burst into floods of tears.

"Jack Sharpe? Now I know 'tis a trick. What harm could Jack do anyone? If he was here you must have been mistaken in his intentions. He wouldn't hurt you. Why should he? And anyway, he isn't here now." Jordon tried to prise her hands away from his clothing as he spoke. "I have more important things to attend to than playing your silly games . . ."

Even as he uttered the words the sounds of violence penetrated the woods. Wild and blasphemous curses were mingled with threats and deep growls of laughter. Grabbing Benedicta's arm he dragged her to the edge of the trees and stood holding her, forgetting she was there as the play was acted out beside the cottage below them. Further along, Jack Sharpe crept silently to see what was going on. His mouth dropped open as he dribbled down his smock, his eyes wide and all thoughts of fornication fled.

"A rat in his hole!" Thomas Fytton had the unfortunate Banaster in his grip, one hand holding a large clump of the tangerine-coloured hair, which he pulled forcefully with every word.

"A pig ripe for sticking," Rob Holland grinned. "Or is that too great an insult to pigs?"

"By God, the King shall hear . . ." Adam Banaster struggled against his fate.

"The King? The King shall hear . . . what?" Thomas's face was barely an inch from that of his captive. He cleared his throat and spat the opaque phlegm into the freckled features. "Rather, Lancaster shall hear! Your revolt, little man, is over. Your moment of glory, gone for ever. And your precious King will not lift a finger . . . unless to shove it up his own arse!"

Rob Holland laughed aloud at that, lifting his shortsword to point it at the turncoat's throat. With a deft flick of the wrist it broke the skin. The prisoner winced and Thomas tightened his grip. Again the sword was raised. Again it nicked the skin. Blood trickled down onto the white shirt.

"'Tis fancy garb for a man lying in a cot," Rob wiped the blade on the linen. "Stolen, I'll warrant."

Banaster didn't bother to argue. "For Christ's sake! Take me to Lancaster, if that's what you intend. I'll make my peace with him. Not you!"

"You'd better make your peace with one higher even than Lancaster," Fytton chuckled. "Though we can't wait for you to confess all your sins or we'd be here until tomorrow!" With a sudden jerk of his arm he brought Banaster to his knees in the dust. Holland sliced the edge of the sword through the windpipe. Blood gushed out.

"Too late. I fear you must go unshriven." The thick red liquid bubbled onto the blade before spattering the garden path. And again the point pierced the flesh. This time behind the ear. Adam Banaster's eyes rolled upwards in his agony, only the whites showing, a fine network of veins bulging from the glossy surface. The final rush of air from gasping lungs flecked the two tormentors with a delicate spray of scarlet spume.

"We'll use the stone." Robert Holland indicated the block once used by Ralph Dane to sharpen his knives. "Stretch his neck on that."

Jordon and Benedicta watched in silence, he, savouring every move, she, horror-struck at the sight. And Jack Sharpe slid from his hiding-place and ran as fast as he could back to Gawsworth Hall. He couldn't wait to tell Mistress Petronilla! Her lover's head was severed from its body!

"That'll show others what becomes of any trying to undermine the power of the Hollands! An example, and one that's long overdue!" Robert Holland's success under Lancaster had resulted in his becoming first a knight and then a baron and being put in charge of Chester, Rhuddlan and Flint Castles. Banaster and his neighbours had let jealousy carry them into one indiscretion too many. Sir Henry Lea was later caught and executed in Manchester, though Sir William Bradshaigh escaped into exile, leaving his wife and family behind. And Banaster's final escapade left a small tragedy in its wake.

6

"OH, you should have seen what I have seen! You should have seen it!" Jack Sharpe didn't wait to enlighten Tilda any more than that he shot in through the kitchen door and across the earth floor. In a second he had disappeared through into the Hall, despite the fact that he was only allowed there if there was a job for him to do.

"Come back here, Jack Sharpe!" Tilda knew she was wasting her breath by the silly excited grin on the lad's face. "What have you seen?" She sighed. Nothing very special, as like as not. The boy was too fanciful for words.

He took the stairs two at a time, calling as he ran. "Mistress Petronilla! Mistress Petronilla!" If she wasn't in the Hall, which she wasn't, then she must be in Mistress Isabel's solar, he reasoned. He'd never been in there, but that wasn't going to stop him today. He'd burst if he wasn't the first to tell her the news.

In the upper solar, Petronilla had combed Isabel's long, heavy tresses and was binding them under the fresh white coif. She was late today. Isabel had been tardy about her tasks and kept her maid with her longer than normal. Haste only made Petronilla clumsy and she had already had three attempts at the headdress by the time they heard Jack calling as he ran.

The door burst open and Isabel rose stiffly to her feet. "What do you mean by this, Jack? You know you are not allowed into my room." Her voice was stern, stopping him in his tracks. Pray to God the imbecile wasn't about to impart the news she had been hoping to break gently to her maid.

"It's 'im, Mistress. Done for, he is!" Jack spoke to Petronilla, not his Mistress.

"Jack! Get out of my room. I shall speak to you later . . . " Isabel tried to stop him with her authority.

"Done for?" Petronilla tried to make some sense out of his ramblings. "Who is done for?" She moved across the creaking wooden floor towards him, intending to pinch his ear and send him back to the kitchen. "You're talking more nonsense than usual, lad."

"'Tisn't nonsense!" Jack was indignant. "I saw it. They pricked him first and let him spurt a while. Then they cut his throttle and he bubbled. And then they took his head. Hacked it off across the knife-stone by the door." He smiled triumphantly.

The maid stopped where she was, her hand still raised to nip him. Jack was too stupid to invent a tale like that. But if he was telling the truth . . . As she felt Isabel's comforting arm around her shoulder she knew he didn't lie. Who the culprits were, she couldn't guess. Why they should do such a thing, she had no idea. But that Adam was dead, she was no longer in any doubt. With a small moan Petronilla tore herself away from Isabel and ran headlong down the steep, ladder-like stair, almost tripping over her skirts.

"Petronilla! Wait!" Isabel followed her, pushing Jack roughly out of her way as she passed. "And if you've a brain at all in that skull, you'll make yourself scarce," she called over her shoulder.

Jack scratched his head. What had he done wrong this time? He'd have thought they wanted to know.

Geoffrey Bernulf arrived at the cottage slightly out of breath. He had gone directly to the cross-roads at the end of Gallows Field from the Hall, knowing that Holland and Fytton were most likely to take the remains of their victim to be hung in full view as a reminder to others of the results of treachery. He had not been wrong. The rest of the hunting party had made their way to the same spot and so it was before a small crowd that the body of Adam Banaster of Lancashire was hung upside down by its feet from the gibbet, the headless corpse still dripping gore onto the stones below.

"Take note, good men and true!" Thomas Fytton reached into the blood-stained bag hanging from his saddle and dragged the severed head into the fading light. The eyes were still rolled upwards under the open lids, only the bulging whites visible to the onlookers. The wide mouth sagged, congealed blood seeming to fill the cavity with a dark-red jelly. Thomas held the trophy high, his square fingers hidden by the still-bright tangerine curls. "Should any one of you think to cross your Master, you may be sure that Adam here will make room for you alongside. Isn't it right, Mister Banaster?" The grin he gave left the men in no doubt that he spoke the truth. Nor any doubt that he would enjoy nothing more than to carry out the sentence himself. They turned away silently, taking their several ways home. None was completely innocent. The odd rabbit here. The bit of kindling there. They knew there was little to fear from Mistress Isabel. But the Fyttons were quite another matter. And Thomas was the last one anyone would wish to cross.

After watching the two men ride away to present Banaster's head to the Earl of Lancaster, Geoffrey had run most of the way back. Sooner or later, Petronilla would have to know what had happened. Any way. Not only had she been used. She had been used by the man who had murdered her husband. It was almost dusk now and at first he couldn't make out the figures standing on the cottage path.

"Jordon?" It was his son. And Benedicta. The girl was as white as a ghost and by the look of her and the stains on the front of her dress she had been vomiting.

"We saw it all." Jordon nodded at Benedicta. "I've tried to explain, but I don't think she understands the reasons. It's as though she is asleep."

"And Petronilla?" Geoffrey carefully unclenched the girl's fists where they clung to Jordon's shirt.

"I haven't seen her." Jordon brushed his clothing, glad to be free at last.

At that moment footsteps could be heard, pounding along the path beside the wood, coming from the direction of the Hall, and through the gloom the figure of Mistress Dane approached. Her face was red with the exertion and her hair dishevelled, escaping from the headdress in wiry strands. Sweat beaded her upper lip and soaked through the stuff of her dress, leaving large dark stains under her armpits. She ignored, or didn't see, the three people standing there. Her eyes searched the ground. And all the time she moaned softly to herself, like a child trying to understand a beating. Two paces from the door of her little home, she stopped. There it was. Jack hadn't lied. The ground was slippery with his blood. The knife-stone slicked with the same red gloss. And there, still pink, was a sliver of flesh, cut away by the sword as it hacked at his neck. Petronilla didn't feel a thing, but her knees gave way beneath her and she fell in a dead faint, lying ungainly in the pools of blood.

They had taken her in and laid her on the bed-sacks before her eyelids flickered and Petronilla awakened to face the nightmare.

"Thomas gloried in it," Geoffrey was whispering. "And there was more than just an idle threat in the words he used before he left."

"Threat?" Isabel felt her own throat constrict. It must feel like that when the rope tightened.

"Aye. After this Fytton and Holland will not be able to do wrong in Lancaster's eyes. Banaster's head is their licence to kill any they take a dislike to. All they need do is cry treason."

"Oh . . . " Petronilla groaned as reality

seeped through her muddled thoughts.

"Hush now." Isabel wiped the sweat from her maid's brow. "Jordon has gone to fetch Christiana and her potions. She will help you to sleep." And bring Benedicta back from her strange waking dream, she hoped.

"But why? He was a good man..." Petronilla tried to sit up. "Who killed him?"

"We were all fooled by him." Geoffrey got to his feet. If Fytton and Holland hadn't done it, he would have. "Tell her." He squeezed Isabel's hand protectively. It would come more sympathetically from another woman, and the archer was too astute to be there when Christiana arrived. If he made himself absent their only concern would be Petronilla, but if he stayed, the two women in his life would see themselves as rivals for his attention. And that was something he had avoided carefully for years.

By the time Isabel had told Petronilla the whole story of Adam Banaster's treachery, Christiana Marton had arrived, busying herself in the preparation of a sleeping draught. Henbane. That potent herb of the meadow. Too much, and the patient would never wake again. The witch-woman tried to concentrate. This was Petronilla's tragedy, but the horror it had released could so easily carry others to their deaths. Their masters now had *carte blanche* ... She glanced at the Mistress of Gawsworth through the corner of her eye. Did the woman love Geoffrey as much as she herself did? Could that love make Isabel see sense and send him away from her bed once and for all? If she didn't, then God help them ...

"May He forgive me, for I shall never forgive myself!" Petronilla was but an empty shadow of the woman she had been only one short year before. Now there was a terrible despair in her eyes. A hopelessness.

"You were not to know ... " The words sounded inadequate, even to Isabel's own ears.

"I betrayed him! Ralph ... !" The maid sobbed loudly, every breath threatening to shake her apart. "How could I? And with Banaster, of all men ... ?"

"Here. Take this." Christiana offered

her friend the cup. "It will calm you. Soothe you."

"Nothing can soothe me but the balm of death. My crime will forever laugh in my face. Taunting me . . ." She saw the concern of the women bending over her and her voice fell to a desolate whisper. "My punishment is too great to be borne." Her eyes grew wide with horror. "I am with child!"

In silence Christiana lifted the cup once more to Petronilla's mouth and held it there until the contents were all swallowed. Isabel stroked the fevered brow, hoping her own horror was hidden. Why had this woman been singled out for such a fate? What had she ever done to deserve it? As though reading her mind Ralph Dane's widow answered her question.

"In all the years we were man and wife I never gave him a moment's peace nor a kind word. He only heard harsh words from my tongue. How I scolded! How I nagged! And God in His wisdom has seen fit to show me the error of my ways . . ." Her voice faded as the medicine began to work. The mouth, drooped with sadness, continued to move, but no words could be distinguished. The eyelids slowly closed and the breathing became easier. Regular. And Petronilla slept. Benedicta had also succumbed to the strength of the drug and slept peacefully on the hearth. Isabel lifted her carefully and laid her beside the now quiet form of her mother.

"I shall stay here tonight," Christiana told her. "In case they wake before morning. Or Petronilla could take it into her head to make an end of herself . . ."

Isabel sighed and sat down on the stool by the hearth as the other woman made a tisane of purslane sweetened with honey. Then together they sat in uneasy silence as they sipped the soothing drink, each with their thoughts centred on one man. Strong. Dark. Handsome. Geoffrey Bernulf. Archer. Thatcher. And poacher. But most of all, Geoffrey Bernulf the lover. And of the two, it was Mistress Isabel who felt the more apprehensive.

Christiana spoke first, her blue eyes wide with anxiety as she put the question uppermost in her mind to the Lady of the Manor. Her rival.

"Do you love him?" She hesitated

as Isabel gasped, astonished by her forthright attitude. Christiana leaned forward, determined to continue. "Do you love him enough to let him go, Mistress?"

"Love him? Who?" Isabel found it difficult to let go the pretence, never mind the man. She had never openly admitted her passion for the peasant to anyone, save Petronilla. Others, like Christiana and some of his friends from Macclesfield, might guess, but as long as she never mentioned it, never showed by a look or a word all that had taken place between them, then no one could ever know for sure. And if ever she was accused of fornication, she would deny it to the last breath of her body.

"You know who I mean, Mistress. It is time we stopped playing games." Christiana reached out and laid her hand on the other woman's arm. "His life is at stake."

The silence after those words had been spoken seemed to last a lifetime. His life? What did the witch-woman mean? Isabel stared at her. "His life?" She sounded bemused.

Christiana glanced across at the sleeping Petronilla and her daughter. "Banaster crossed Thomas Fytton." There was no need to say more.

Isabel's mind raced. It was true. Her mother and her stepfather had put the proposal to her the minute Sir John was safe in his coffin and she had protested her grief so strongly that they had to let her be. But the situation would not be tolerated for much longer. She knew that. And she had been giving herself headaches wondering how best to go about the marriage Geoffrey had lived for since that first time they met, at Barnaby Fair. How could it be arranged? Not at Gawsworth, that was certain. And with Hugh Fytton rector of most of the churches in the area she had been at something of a loss, the ideas becoming less and less practical as each was discarded. She had been living in a dream world, as he had for years. She had accepted his fantasy, believing in its colours and designs. Yet it was simply a rainbow. A beautiful rainbow with a crock of gold at the end. But that end was impossible to find. The crock of gold the stuff of fairy-tales . . .

"Let him go, Mistress. Do not condemn him to death, I beg you. If you love him . . ." Christiana had tears in her eyes. "I love him too. I shall take care of him. I swear it."

Isabel looked at Petronilla, and then at the crippled woman still holding her arm. A silent sob shook her body from head to foot. Why? Why, when after all the youthful years of passion, and the sterile years before she realised the truth, must it end like this? Their love was deeper than any known on earth. They had survived all manner of trials. All manner of tribulations to get to the point of perfect understanding. She had thought he only wanted Gawsworth. She had thought him only of peasant stock. He had seen her as a challenge. He had thought her haughty in the extreme. Yet they had a son. They should be a family. And there was a feeling between them which could never be taken away. No matter what the world did to them, it would continue for ever. In their hearts. Despite everything, theirs was a true love. And what could Christiana know of that? But ... But she was right. Isabel put her head down into her lap and gave way to tears. They flowed hot and fast, burning the delicate tissue of eye and nose, swelling it until she could hardly breathe. Her skin became blotchy and her lips wet with saliva turned to slime. How could anyone know how she felt? Compared to Christiana she seemed to have so much. The manor. The lands. Married to a Knight ... And yet the blue-eyed woman with the golden hair and the twisted leg had spent her life looking after him. She had cooked for him and washed his clothes. Kept his house, even though that house be nothing better than a rude hovel on the Gawsworth lands. And kept him warm in the long winter nights. She had tended his coughs and mended his shirt and done all the things a woman longed to do for a man. In short, she had loved him. And so Isabel cried all the harder.

"Hush, Mistress." Christiana put her arms around the weeping woman and rocked her gently. "He loves you. I know that for a certainty. His feeling for you is a thing no one on earth can break. He would lie for you. He would steal for you ... He would kill for you! No matter that Fate has seen fit to keep you apart, you have had his heart since he was little more than a boy, and all the Fyttons under the sun cannot take that knowledge away from you. But they can take his life. And they will, if they so much as guess the things he hopes for. There is room for another at the end of Gallows Field, and they'd string him up without fear of retribution."

The truth of Christiana's words tore at Isabel's heart like the jagged edge of a dagger. There was no hope for them. No future for them. It had all been an illusion, built on promises. Promises which could never be fulfilled. But how could she let him go? How could she ever *make* him go? He wanted the dream as much as she did. He would rather die than see her suffer at the hands of Thomas Fytton. Heartbroken and confused, she raised her head to look at Christiana. "You will take care of him ... "

Christiana Marton nodded. "If you can persuade him ... "

Mistress Isabel de Orreby, widow of Sir John Grindon, smiled tightly through her tears. "I turned away from him once before and married another. I was blind and stupid then, thinking that keeping company with kings and princes put me above my own people. And Geoffrey, always the underdog, was willing to be kicked aside by virtue of his burden of inferiority. I can persuade him. It will tear me apart, but for his sake I will do it." She stood, taking the other woman's hand in hers as she did so. "Never believe the part I play. Never think for a single moment that I have stopped loving him, for I never shall whilst there is breath in my body." Isabel paused, squeezing Christiana's fingers and looking deep into the blue eyes which now held the first glimmer of hope. "You will remain here all night? With Petronilla?"

Christiana felt her lower lip tremble. She wanted to protest. And yet she could not. The man she loved loved this woman, and for his sake she would allow Isabel her last goodbye. "I shall stay until dawn. Petronilla will need her friends in the coming months, with a fatherless child to support, and I am more than willing to give her aid." There was a wealth of sadness in her words. What wouldn't she have given to have a child! And if God had been good, there would have been no question of Geoffrey Bernulf straying from her bed. Not even for the Lady of Gawsworth Hall.

★ ★ ★

"How does she fare? Have you given her a draught?" The man on the far side of the room, naked to the waist, glistened with the water he had just washed in. He had his back to the door.

"She sleeps."

"Isabel!" He spun round. "I thought . . ."

"Christiana will stay with her tonight. So I thought . . ." Isabel moved slowly towards him, smiling softly, no trace of the recent tears dimming her emerald eyes. She stood before him and raised her hands to the broad chest, where droplets merged and mingled before running in tiny rivulets down his body. His warmth dispelled the chill of wetness on her palms and the years evaporated. It was all so long ago, when they stood like this on the banks of the Bolyn, and he had made a woman of the girl. Sixteen years. Of lust. And hate. And now . . . love.

A gleam of understanding lit his dark eyes and he lifted her from her feet and kissed her. "You are a wanton, Mistress. And I should beat you for it." But instead, he kissed her again.

"If a wanton is a woman with a mind of her own, then I am guilty and you may drag me to court on law-day to have me fined. But if a wanton is a fornicator, then I am guilty and you may drag me before the church and have me fined." She untied the lace at the side of her gown and lifted the garment over her head as she spoke. She wore nothing underneath except her own still shapely, still supple skin. The breasts were still firm and proud and the waist still tiny above the slight swell of her belly. Pubic hair gleamed as red as the fire which illuminated it. "But if a wanton woman is a woman who loves . . . then you may drag me to the bed and love me." She giggled as the girl she had once been would have giggled.

"Mistress?" He raised a quizzical eyebrow at these carefree antics, but was obviously not dismayed at them.

"Come, slowcoach." Isabel caught hold of his hand and pulled him towards the bed-sacks. With a low chuckle she pushed him down and began to wrestle with the fastenings of his nether garments. In a second or two she had him lying under her as naked as the day he was born. Geoffrey twisted onto one elbow, automatically trying to assume dominance.

"Hey!" he protested as he found himself pressed against the sacks.

"Lie still." Isabel sat astride him, laughing at the surprise on his face. She began to move against him. Gentle, subtle movements. Unhurried. Sensuous. His body thrust itself up to meet her.

"Still, I said." She played with him. As he had played with her. She coaxed him and touched him, laughing all the time. But inside she cried. And silently she prayed. Dear God, let me remember this. Let me remember him until the day I die. Let me remember how he loves me tonight.

For tomorrow, he would hate her.

Geoffrey felt every muscle in his body tremble with exhaustion as Isabel swayed above him. Devouring him. Enclosing him in a rippling sensation in which he was destined to drown. Slowly, imperceptibly, she took him to the point from which there was no return. He stared, mesmerised by the sorceress as she manipulated his acquiescing body; fascinated by the sudden emergence of female authority. He had no resistance. Her hands, her mouth, her body, claimed him. In the final seconds of his ecstasy he clasped her to him as though to blend their souls together for all eternity just as surely as their damp, triumphant bodies blended in the breathless beauty of their last consummation.

It was two hours later when he stirred and wakened from the deep, dreamless sleep of satisfaction to find her watching him, quite unaware that she had observed every breath, every flicker of his eyelids, every twitch of a muscle, in the dying light of the fire. She could feel the fluids with which he had anointed her sticky between her legs and wanted it always to be that way. But this was the last time. She wanted him to sleep beside her always. But he never would again. She wanted him to love her until he died. But he would turn away from her. Isabel wanted to hold him and kiss him and swear that they would be man and wife, but if he was to live out his life as he should, it was impossible. The tears threatening to choke her must be ignored. She could not break now. She could not cry. Instead, she had to laugh and pretend gaiety. Seem flippant and uncaring. She had to hurt him. She had to pretend it had all been a game.

"Have you finished with me now, unvirtuous jade?" He leaned to kiss her parted lips, still luscious from the previous thousand kisses. "If I didn't know you better I'd swear you've been living a secret life to rival that of Mistress Cherry."

"If you didn't know me better?" Isabel chuckled. It began in her elegant white throat as an amused gurgle, emerging seconds later as a side-splitting laugh. She laughed till she cried, holding her sides as they began to ache. "If you didn't know me . . . "

Geoffrey raised himself onto one elbow, nonplussed. The more she laughed, the more baffled and confused he became. Was she laughing at him? Why? Bewilderment became suspicion. "And what does that mean, Mistress?" All drowsiness and contentment had evaporated with her laughter. It sounded like profanity. Almost blasphemy after the love-making she had induced.

"How could you know me? How could you?" She kissed him cheekily on the end of his nose. "You only know what you wish to know. And what I wish you to believe. Is the woman so different from the girl? And didn't the girl come to you willingly on the river bank?" Isabel winked at him. "You and how many more?"

As disbelief turned rapidly to incredulity and then disgust the Mistress of Gawsworth fought a desperate battle with herself, determined not to see the pain she caused. Better this than the Gallows Field. Relentlessly she forced herself to continue, scourging herself with each self-denunciation.

"You only let yourself see Isabel de Orreby. The heiress. The lady. And so saw yourself elevated to lord by my patronage. My sojourn to the delights of London Town and the King's Court only increased your longing." She smiled wickedly. "And added to my repertoire of conquests. But," she leaned towards him, her voice low and seductive, "when I wanted a taste of a real man, I knew I could always count on Bernulf. My archer. My thatcher. My very own peasant."

The palm of his hand hit her face so forcefully that it knocked her head sideways. The return blow with the knuckles was so rapid that she thought her neck broken. Isabel bit her lip, drawing blood, but she never made a sound. She deserved it, and more. The physical pain was but a pin-prick to the mental anguish she suffered. He believed her. He had so little faith. And yet, the lack of faith in her could ultimately save his life.

"Slut!" The word was muttered through clenched teeth. "And Jordon? Do you *know* who fathered your son?"

Isabel swallowed hard and forced a teasing laugh. "A man is never more virile than when angered. But Jordon? Could I ever deny, even to myself, that he is yours? Your hair. Your eyes. Your face. There is so little of me in him that no one has ever guessed who left him at your mother's door, but no one has questioned why! He is yours to the end of his toes!" It was all her fault that Jordon had missed his mother's love, but she would not have him abandoned by his father too. Her present guilt was quite enough to bear.

Geoffrey had turned away, afraid to raise his hand to her again in case he murdered her. It was Lucifer's bad luck that he should choose that moment to rub against the archer's leg. As the foot struck him, knocking the breath from his body, he was lifted from his feet and found himself airborne. Then he fell, like a stone, right into the middle of the still glowing embers. With a screech as evil as the dead rising from the grave, the cat flew at the door, clawing at the wood in a frenzy.

"Get out! Both of you!" Geoffrey

grabbed Isabel by the hair and almost dragged her to the door of the little room. Opening it he flung her out after the howling animal into the deep-blue half-light of the star-strewn summer night.

★ ★ ★

Inside the tavern in Backwallgate below St Michael's Church, Jordon of Bolyn re-read the curling parchment hardly daring to believe the contents. "Edith! Another jug of ale!" Edith Baguley, whose sister Maud had married Dickon Miller, obliged the young customer and his friend with a smile. They were not the usual riff-raff. The foreigner came from London, she was sure. And she knew for a fact that Mister Jordon had himself *spoken* to the King! Her sister had it from her husband, and *he* was a friend of Geoffrey Bernulf, the boy's father, so it must be true. Imagine! Speaking to the King! Her own husband, Tom Pearson, had made a rather more crude interpretation of her sister's tale, but Edith was used to his jaundiced view of life. He'd never been the same since one of the great *destriers* bred just beyond Macclesfield for the Earls to ride in battle, had crippled him. A wasp had stung the horse, and the horse had kicked Tom Pearson. His leg had been smashed and but for old Edmund Fytton slicing the useless limb off with his sword, he'd no doubt have been dead years ago. No. Jordon seemed a very personable young man, Edith thought.

"Tell me again. Who sent you?" Jordon lifted the brimming cup to his lips.

John le Marshal sighed amiably. He'd been through it three times already. "My master sent me. Hugh de Spenser. The younger. The deed had been lodged with King Edward in case the worst should befall Sir John Grindon. As indeed it did, at Bannock Burn."

"As it did," murmured Jordon, remembering that day.

"And Sir John being such a . . . *good friend* of my lord . . . the King entrusted him to see that the deed was carried out."

"So now I am on my way to fulfilling my ambition, despite my confinement to the north-west of the nation. I knew it would come about! I just knew it would!" The cup was emptied and refilled. It was a night to celebrate.

"And you are not alone in that. Since his marriage to Eleanor de Clare, my master has aspirations to the Earldom of Gloucester." John le Marshal grinned. "Though he'll have a fight on his hands from the men now married to her sisters. Gaveston's widow Margaret is now wife to Hugh Audley, and Elizabeth, the youngest, is wife to Roger d'Amory. He's made a good start though. He's already seduced Newport from Audley and has his eye on the Isle of Lundy . . . "

"The Court doesn't change," Jordon chuckled. "A nest of vipers! Dog eat dog! But if de Spenser has thoughts of becoming Earl of Gloucester, *and* taking Wales under his wing, he'd best watch the Marcher Lords. The Mortimers won't take kindly to his schemes!"

"He'll survive!" John drained his cup and held it out to be refilled. "Though as you say, he makes enemies rather than friends. D'Amory seeks the protection of Pembroke, and Audley looks to Lancaster, but . . . " He leaned forward knowingly. "Hugh de Spenser has the King!" He winked.

Jordon nearly spat ale all over Mistress Pearson's hearth. "The King has Hugh de Spenser, don't you mean!" If his laughter was slightly hysterical, he could be forgiven. He was on his way back to London. This time as a man of substance. John Grindon had seen to that. "But," he said more soberly, "what of the house? And Mistress Boundle?"

John slapped his friend on the back. "Don't worry over her. As soon as she heard of Sir John's death, she was after another husband. There was nothing else to be done, knowing that the house was only hers by his bounty. Her greatest disappointment was that he never introduced her to the Court, but now she is to be wed to a butcher from Pudding Lane and will no doubt grow fatter by the minute."

"And Angareta?" Jordon remembered the grey-eyed girl.

"She takes care of the house. Until you arrive. And after, if you wish . . . "

It could have been the over-indulgence of Mistress Edith's ale, or the memories of a willing child, or . . . something else. Jordon blinked the mistiness away. John Grindon had given him the chance he wanted. A house of his own. Not far from the Chepe. In London. It came then, all of a sudden, to Jordon of Bolyn, that it was perhaps wrong to simply *use* people. John Grindon had not done that. John Grindon had loved him, and this parchment was the proof of his love. How selfish he felt. How young and pathetic. If he stretched his imagination he could almost feel the pain he had caused the older man. The way he had smiled at others, ignoring the one to whom he owed most. The way he had used him to further his own ends. The way he had stood and watched him die. On the battlefield. At Bannock Burn.

And Jordon wept at last for the love he had not recognised.

* * *

"Mistress? May I?" Christiana stood diffidently on the threshold of the upper room.

"Of course." Isabel's smile as she

greeted the witchwoman was empty of all happiness. She had sat stoically as Petronilla braided her hair before slipping the bridal gown over her mistress's head, and had been gazing into space, ignoring the 'oohs' and 'aahs' emanating at regular intervals from her mother's lips as she admired the prettily concocted crespine of pale ruched net and gauze. She cared nothing for the silk bows and medallions. If they had dressed her in sack-cloth and ashes she would scarcely have noticed.

"Mother." She suddenly addressed Cecily as though the older woman was irritating her. "Shouldn't you check on Tilda? To make sure that the feast is being properly prepared?"

"Don't you worry, my dear. 'Tis only wedding nerves making you tetchy, but to put your mind at rest I shall go and inspect the meats." Humming a little tune to herself, Mistress Fytton left the younger woman alone, her face alight with the pleasure of a long cherished dream fulfilled.

"Myrtle and rosemary for your bouquet." Christiana held out the fresh, pungent herbs. Her voice was soft; her eyes full of sympathy. She could only admire the Lady of Gawsworth Hall for her selflessness and courage in giving up the man she so loved, but she admired her more for the courage she showed in giving herself to Thomas Fytton. In doing that, she must know that Geoffrey Bernulf would give up any tiny lingering hope he might have had, despite his protestations. Mistress Marton didn't know how Isabel had achieved her aim, but somehow she had made the archer hate her. He would not have her name mentioned. In the week since Adam Banaster had lost his head, Geoffrey had thrown himself into a frenzy of work, dragging young Francis Miller after him for miles in search of the materials he needed for his building.

As Isabel accepted the gift, Petronilla sniffed noisily. Mistress Isabel had been so kind to her, insisting that Petronilla was still needed at the Hall and that the marriage to Thomas would make not one bit of difference as far as she was concerned. *If* the maid could see her way fit to being in Mister Fytton's company! Once she had been acquainted with the full facts of the case she could see that there had been no choice in the matter. Banaster had been a traitor and had met no worse an end than he deserved. And she counted herself very fortunate to have employment still and friends who were prepared not to shun her for her mistakes. But what of Isabel? And what of Geoffrey Bernulf? Christiana seemed at last about to achieve her heart's desire. Once Isabel was married to Thomas, there would be no reason on earth why Geoffrey could not take her to wife at last and make an honest woman of her.

"Ohhh, Mistress . . . " Petronilla wailed softly. Thomas Fytton was not the man for so kind a woman. He was rough. A soldier. The furthest thing from that refined courtier Sir John Grindon that anyone could imagine. He didn't have the slightest feeling for Isabel. It was only for the Hall and the estate.

"There is no time for regrets. It has to be. And I ask you now never to mention, or even think of, the things that have gone before. They never happened. Is that understood?" There was a new sternness and authority to Isabel's voice. A hardness. A barrier had been raised between her and her past and she looked now only to the future as the wife of the man who at this moment waited for her inside the little church beside the Hall.

* * *

The ceremony, the feast and the frolics accompanying Isabel's change in status were as different as could be imagined from the events of her previous marriage. This time the ale and wine flowed for hours so that by the end of the evening every man in the place had the greatest difficulty standing, and many of the women were in similar state. Only Isabel remained sober. Wine would not prevent the evening turning into night. It could not stop the inevitable. Next year she would be thirty years old and in all those years she had never been touched by anyone but Geoffrey Bernulf. She remembered how, when they were young and foolish, she had promised that she would never lie with another. She had come close to breaking that promise when she had married Sir John, but fate had decreed otherwise and allowed her to return to her true love. But this time there could be no escape. This time she was breaking that promise to save the man she was turning her back on.

Now, the last of the revellers were leaving. The crude remarks and obscenities and the hysterical laughter were fading, and only Petronilla was left, her hand on the latch of the bedroom chamber door and such a miserable look on her face that it might have been a funeral.

"I think your maid is in love with me," Thomas laughed as he slid his arms around his new wife. "Well?" He looked at the hovering woman. "Either close the door behind you or come and join us. I've taken half-a-dozen on a good night, so two will be no problem . . ."

"Ohhh! Ohhh! Mistress . . ." Petronilla could control herself no longer and burst into tears before turning away and slamming the oak door behind her.

Thomas shrugged his shoulders. Women were impossible to understand so he saw no point in even trying. They did, however, have their uses and Sir John's widow was no doubt eagerly awaiting the end of her enforced chastity, caused by the unfortunate death of her previous husband. And Roger de Macclesfield, the man she had first been betrothed to, had been murdered before he even got the chance to bed her at all! Poor lady. She had been sadly lacking in luck when it came to lovers! But now he was about to put an end to her misery. He turned to her, his left arm under her shoulders. With one sharp movement Thomas tore the linen shift from her neck to waist and took her left breast in his hand, squeezing and kneading it before lowering his head to bite the dark protruding nipple.

Isabel froze. Her fists clenched. Her toes curled. And every muscle in her body seemed to turn to iron. She wanted to scream. She wanted to fight. To kick and punch and scratch. But she could not. He was her husband. He had a right to her body. He owned it. She closed her eyes and tried not to think. Tried to ignore the things he was doing to her. Every inch of skin shivered under the investigation of his fingers as they found and tested the places only Geoffrey had been privy to until tonight.

"Mistress?" Thomas paused as he

recognised hostility. For a moment he had thought he was once more enjoying the spoils of war rather than consummating a marriage. He looked down on the closed face of his wife. She didn't move. Didn't speak. She made no effort to bring him pleasure or fulfil her wifely duties.

Isabel heard the question in the word. But she smelt the rancid wine on his breath and the stale sweat under his arms. And as he threw the blanket back to expose her to full view she was engulfed by the even more pungent odours of piss and ordure. God help her! What had she done? But even as those thoughts came into her mind she knew she had done the right thing. This man would have killed Geoffrey if he had known the peasant had ideas of becoming the master of Gawsworth. He would have done it without hesitation. And never given it another thought. Thomas Fytton was a man who believed in getting what he wanted, and if he had to kill or maim in the attempt, then so much the better. Bernulf the archer would have been nothing more than a minor nuisance and disposed of in a minute. She prayed silently. "Geoffrey. Forgive me. If not in this world, then in the next."

Thomas Fytton had eaten and drunk his fill at the feast and had eyed this woman with anticipation. Fine breasts. A firm little arse. And a face which was somehow still virginal, despite her years and the fact that she had been married before. And now she was acting the virgin! It was a neat trick, and one he hadn't expected. But if that was what she wanted, then he was the man to oblige.

He tore the linen bed-gown to shreds, chuckling as he did so.

Then he was on her, stretching out her arms and pinning them to the bed, forcing open her thighs with his hard-muscled legs and her mouth with his probing, lascivious tongue. She struggled. Then she fought and twisted in an effort to avoid the pain. But even as she gasped for air through his saliva she felt herself torn apart by his savage onslaught. His ragged nails tore at her tender flesh and his teeth drew blood, and as he pounded her remorselessly, grunting and gasping with the force of his own brutality, she felt the weight of her guilt leaving her. The degradation cleansed her. The ruthless cruelty was balm to her troubled soul. It was what she deserved. Her punishment for the pain she had caused and the destruction of everything her lover had once held so dear. She had given him his freedom at last. Defiled and debased as she now was, Geoffrey Bernulf would never have the slightest desire to make love to her again.

7

"DON'T dawdle, boy! And take care with those ledgers!" Jordon de Bolyn adjusted his fur-collared long-coat more comfortably about his shoulders as they turned the corner into Lombardy Street. At twenty years of age he was tall and athletic with a head of dark, unruly curls and the elegance and assurance to match any of the young courtiers at King Edward's Court. Yet he was as well known for his prowess with the sword and lance at the tournaments as he was for his gallantry and chivalry to the fairer sex. He had unseated as many accomplished knights as he had seduced lovely ladies, and where the men found his humour and cheerfulness an attraction, the women could not help but try to fathom the strange soulfulness behind the sometimes brooding blackness of his eyes. He nursed a secret. An inner pain. And after they had loved him they were always left with the feeling that they had failed. They could not heal the wound from which his heart bled. Yet, if the man brooded he did not recognise the fact. He thought he had put it behind him, and if ever his mind wandered back to the days of childhood it was only to dwell on the place itself. The forests, hills and rolling meadows of Cheshire. Occasionally, he admitted, he was homesick. He believed he had come to terms with Isabel de Orreby's treachery in marrying Fytton, not Bernulf, in the light of events of recent years.

"Come on, boy! In! And put the parchments on the table." Jordon stood aside to let Hodge Pearson past. It was fully four years now since he had been persuaded by Edith the alewife to take her youngest son out into the great wide world to make his fortune, as she put it. As well he might have done, if he had possessed a single shred of ambition. But unfortunately, although he did as he was told, he never looked further. Never saw an opportunity. Never pushed himself. Unless it was in the pursuit of pleasure. Hodge Pearson was renowned throughout the city for his unbeatable skill at sling-shot and his unfailing aim in the game of quoits, and amongst the apprentices and scufflers he had become a household name. Such expertise required a great deal of practice and gave a good indication of the way the lad spent his time, which was hardly what his mother Edith had had in mind. Still, she had done her best for her son. And Jordon de Bolyn knew that his own mother was now trying to make up to him for the omissions of the past.

"Angareta!" The room was empty, though the fire burned on the hearth. Jordon walked across the stone floor and pushed open the door to the kitchen. The young woman hadn't heard him enter and stood, one hand pressed to the small of her back to ease the ache as she basted the shoulder of lamb. The distended belly under the folds of her grey wool dress showed that she was very near her time.

"Jordon." Her face lit up as she turned. He worked so hard, and often he forgot the world outside his trading empire. Sometimes he forgot to come home at all.

"I see your mother has been again." He nodded at the piece of meat. Avelina Boundle called regularly to make sure that the house was not neglected, though she had made no bones about the fact that she thought her daughter was. Big with child, and not yet married! That kind of thing might be acceptable in the rustic north, but Mister Bolyn should have the grace to adopt the ways of the town if he intended staying there! And it was a good thing her husband the butcher didn't mind her taking some of his profits to help Angareta on the days when Jordon 'forgot' to provide!

"And how is life in Pudding Lane?" He dropped a kiss on the top of Angareta's head. "Still awash with innards and gore?" The lane was aptly named, most of the 'puddings' from the slaughtered beasts finding their way into the central gutter of the street, making the whole place reek of rotting guts and making walking a difficult business. Jordon didn't wait for her to answer. "I have work to do. Papers to go over. Accounts to check. We can eat later . . . " He saw the look of disappointment on her face. "But Hodge is here. You can feed him, if that will keep you happy for a while."

It was three hours later that Jordon finally pushed the last of the papers away and leaned back to stretch his shoulders. He was satisfied. Mistress Isabel, wife of Thomas Fytton, had once more provided all she had promised, and at the right price. Wool was now the main export out of London, and Jordon de Bolyn was the main exporter. He smiled to himself. And the chances were that the lamb brought as a gift to his house had been bought from him in the first place by Avelina's husband. His plans were working to perfection and he had to admit, some of the praise had to go to his mother. His mother! He still could not call her Mother, nor ever would be able to. Not unless he wanted to ruin her reputation and bring bloodshed to the Manor of Gawsworth. But of late he had nothing but admiration for that lady. She was tough, and from all he had heard, had become strict and fierce since her marriage to Mister Fytton. She had demanded to be allowed to run the estates, and had somehow got her way, and she had increased the profits for her husband threefold. It was rumoured that the reeve and bailiff walked in dread of her, almost fearing for their lives if there was the smallest discrepancy in the accounts. Jordon chuckled. It seemed that his mother had found her vocation late in life, but it erased any lingering doubts he might have had about his parentage. He had never taken after his father, Bernulf. But there was obviously a lot of Isabel de Orreby in him. That was one of the reasons he had decided to become known as *de* Bolyn. It was easier to make one's way if it was thought that one's ancestry could be traced to a member of King William's conquering army. Foreign traders and Londoners alike assumed that his family had originated in Boulogne and that, in common with most names, the pronunciation had become distorted. Indeed, he answered to a variety of corruptions every day. Bolyn. Bollin. Bouloyn. Even Bullen. He didn't mind. Just so long as the deals the foreigners made were lining *his* pockets. And they were. As were his friends in Court. He exported wool, but he imported a great deal more, and members of the King's household were always willing to purchase rare and exotic luxuries in an effort to enhance their lives.

"I'll say one thing for your mother," Jordon commented, wiping his mouth on the cloth provided. "She can choose a tasty piece of meat."

Angareta smiled her thanks at his kind words. It didn't take much to make her smile, though mostly she cried. She had been in love with Jordon since the first time he came to stay with her mother, in the days when Mistress Isabel was waiting to marry Sir John. It had only been a matter of days before they were tumbling in the orchard at the back of the house. When her mother was safely out of the way gossiping, of course. And then Jordon had come to the arrangement by which they met at the George, on the Chepe. She had been his willing slave, doing anything and everything he asked. And he had asked a lot.

"I shall bring fruit . . . " She staggered a little as she rose from the chair, the cramp in her back making her gasp.

"No. No need. I must be away . . . "

Jordon had no sooner got the words out of his mouth than there was a knock at the door. John le Marshal entered.

"Ah." He welcomed Hugh de Spenser's squire. "News?" The other man nodded. "Bring us ale, Angareta. It might be best if we discuss the matter here rather than be overheard elsewhere."

"I agree." John le Marshal sat down on the seat vacated by the young woman. "Lancaster has more support here at Westminster than he had either at Pontefract or York. This morning he stood and demanded outrageous privileges for the Steward of England, insisting that he be responsible for all manner of new administrations, even to having the power to dismiss negligent officials and councillors." John took a long drink of the ale. "These demands were met quietly, but they were only an opening for his real purpose."

"De Spenser." Jordon had expected as much. "It has been inevitable since last year when Edward commanded the Marcher Lords to keep the peace and Hugh refused to place himself in Lancaster's custody."

"Aye. He might be imprudent, but he isn't a fool," John agreed. "And whilst the arguments were gathering momentum, I made myself useful in the corridors, saying little but listening. And it was worth the effort. My information is that all the Marcher Lords, Hereford, Damory, Audley *and* the Mortimers, have armed men already on the road and marching. Lancaster is making his stand. I'd swear to it, and the King will need every supporter in London before the week is out."

"Then let's away. To Westminster . . . Angareta!"

Angareta Boundle entered the room immediately, her face pale and her heart pounding. If there was going to be civil war she didn't want Jordon caught up in the middle of it all. Not now. With the baby due any day.

"Ah. There you are. I'm away to the King as there may be some small trouble, so don't expect me home. I shall make arrangements nearer the Palace. And stay indoors. Just to be safe. Is Hodge still here?" Jordon was putting on his jerkin over the dagger fastened to his belt. Then he strapped on a short-sword before slipping his arms into the sleeves of his fur-collared long-coat. He still looked every inch the prosperous merchant. The steel was hidden.

"Aye. He's here. Sleeping in the kitchen while he waits your orders." Angareta held on to the edge of the table to try to stop the shaking in her limbs.

"Then keep him with you. If you need anything from outside, send Hodge." He turned to follow John to the door. "And before I come home I shall try to send a message, but only if it is safe to do so." Then the door closed behind the two men and the abandoned woman sat heavily on the chair, laid her head on her arms across the table and broke her heart.

It was only an hour later that Hodge Pearson was awakened to the sound of her screams as she fought to give birth to her first child.

★ ★ ★

Jordon was lucky. With so many comings and goings, it hadn't been difficult to find a corner of a bed-chamber in the Palace of Westminster itself. A bribe to the under-steward and a few coins to a boy to prevent another from usurping his space, and he was in with the household. And by the rumblings and growlings in the corridors, King Edward was in need of as many of his friends as he could gather around him. As John le Marshal had predicted, the Marcher Lords had arrived, determined to intimidate the King, and had cut him off in the Palace by force of arms from his military supplies in the Tower of London. Hugh de Spenser had brought their anger down not only on himself by his avarice, but on Edward too. Jordon and John were both too young to have been involved in the affairs surrounding the King and Piers Gaveston, but the older members of the household couldn't help but make comparisons. Hugh and Edward were very close companions, and de Spenser had been well rewarded.

"What news today?" Jordon had brought a jug of ale and cups to a small antechamber not far from the King's rooms.

"My master is with him now." John raised his cup in salute. "But earlier, after Edward had refused Lancaster's demands, Queen Isabella was admitted and I have it from one of her ladies that she didn't mince her words." He grinned at Jordon. "She'll not bed with a sodomite! Can you imagine her? Belly swollen with yet another. Two princes and a princess still living, and several laid to rest, and she has the nerve to call the King a sodomite!"

"Mayhap they're not all his." Though Jordon knew full well that a man could love a man and still have a number of offspring. Not all were like Sir John Grindon. He thought briefly of Angareta. "Maybe not. Perhaps she takes a leaf from Alice de Lacy's book."

Lancaster's wife, after secretly having an *affaire* with a young squire, Ebulo L'Estrange, for several years, had finally left her husband to live with her lover. "But her argument carried little weight. Then Pembroke tried. Using a similar direction, but reminding Edward of the power of the barons before finishing with the words: He perishes on the rocks that loves another more than himself. Meaning of course, Hugh de Spenser."

"The power of the barons," Jordon repeated thoughtfully. "They are certainly a force to be reckoned with, and with Lancaster leading them . . . " He fell silent. When it came to a war, who would be victorious? Would Lancaster ultimately wear the crown of England?

It was only two weeks later that judgement was given against Hugh de Spenser in Parliament and he was sentenced to banishment, but by that time, Hodge Pearson had managed to track down the whereabouts of Jordon de Bolyn, bringing him the news. Angareta Boundle had died in her vain attempts to part with the child. The baby, a boy, had been as dead as its mother when the midwife had at last slit open the belly to release it into the world. And Avelina, the butcher's wife, had taken charge of the remains of her daughter and grandson and had them decently interred at the Church of All Hallows, by the Tower.

Jordon stood pensively in the tiny bedchamber they had shared and looked out at the orchard. Apples were ripening and the long grass beneath the trees rippled in the warm wind as it subtly changed from green to gold. Poor Angareta. It was there, lying in that grass that he had first shown her the delights of love. Love? Did he know the meaning of the word? Then he shrugged and turned away. She had loved him, and if she was happy loving him, he supposed that was all that mattered. But it was lonely without her. He had to admit it. Returning to the room downstairs he was surprised to find that he had visitors. John le Marshal stood deferentially at his master's shoulder, his lip curled in the smile of a conspirator. Hugh de Spenser pushed back the lock of fair hair which habitually fell across his brow. It was an oft-repeated action. Then he came forward, his hand held out in greeting.

"Jordon. Forgive this unannounced intrusion, but from the things John tells me I believe there are certain matters which can be resolved to our mutual benefit."

Jordon de Bolyn immediately played the host, never for a moment showing the amazement he felt at the honour of this visit. Hugh de Spenser, here, in his house! These were troubled times, and it was in times like these that fortunes could be made. If one was on one's toes! "Pray, be seated, and excuse me for a moment whilst I find us some refreshment."

Hugh de Spenser removed his gloves and the light cape from around his shoulders and sat at the oak board, its surface dull now through lack of attention. Neither Jordon nor Hodge Pearson knew what the soft ball of bee's wax in the kitchen should be used for. Nor were they worried.

"Here we are." Jordon placed yesterday's bread and three slices of cheese on the board. Hodge followed with the last of the ale. Considering his master had more than enough gold lining his pockets, they lived extremely frugally, though the lad knew quite well that it was on account of Mister Jordon being forgetful rather than mean.

"So . . . ?" Jordon was too inquisitive to eat.

"So . . . !" Hugh tapped the oak with his manicured nails. "You have contacts at the port. Ships' Captains? English and foreign? Merchant vessels which could be put to other uses, and make even greater profits?"

"Aye." Jordon began to see the plan.

"I've no mind to scurry off into exile just to appease Lancaster. Edward may be right in avoiding war, but there will be confrontation before we are through and I've no intention of missing it. I'll be my own master, and go where I please. With your help."

"Piracy?" Jordon chuckled. "There are profits to be made, at someone else's expense . . . "

"And you'd get your share." Hugh leaned forward. "I'm not the man to sit on my arse twiddling my thumbs in some foreign backwater when I could be putting my time and energy to better use. Can you find me a ship?"

Jordon didn't even pause to think. "Aye. And a good one. Lean and fast, and with a Dutch crew who have known . . . shall we say, profiteering, before. But on one condition."

"Yes?" Hugh waited.

"That you leave my flag alone! I don't

mind receiving free imports, but I'll not lose my export trade!"

The three men laughed and the bargain was made. Jordon de Bolyn was a contented man. Everything he touched seemed to turn to gold. Except his private life. He nodded thoughtfully to himself. This house was too empty. And it was at that moment that he decided it was time to take a trip on the road to the north. To Gawsworth.

★ ★ ★

"Your servant, Mistress." Jordon bowed over the hand of Isabel Fytton, Lady of the Manor. The minute she had come into his presence in the great hall he had seen the difference in her. She was more assured. More confident, not in the flamboyant way of the Court, but with a calm aura of authority, her back straight and her head high. He felt shaken by her scrutiny, feeling that she saw all his flaws in a moment as the green eyes flashed over his clothes and the person they covered before boring into his soul.

"Sir." Isabel acknowledged her son

with the barest nod of her head. He was handsome. Slightly taller than . . . his father. But with the same strength, physically. She could only hope that in other matters he had avoided the weakness which had been Bernulf's downfall. Did this young man have more than just the vision? Did he have the strength of character to carry through his ambition?

"Hold, Sir! Or I shall run you through!" the lisping voice tried to sound fierce as its owner waved the wooden sword around in the air.

Isabel smiled then and Jordon's heart missed a beat. He knew who the boy must be. And he knew why the woman smiled.

"This," she said, "is Thomas. My son."

Despite the uncomfortable flash of jealousy, Jordon couldn't help laughing. Thomas Fytton the younger had nothing of his father in him. He was a de Orreby through and through with his thick chestnut hair and green eyes and a hint of freckles about his nose, and seemed about to slay the intruder.

"Thomas!" The one word was enough to stop him in his tracks. "Show your respect for Mister Jordon de Bolyn, a friend of King Edward and an even dearer friend of mine."

The boy's eyes opened wide and he quickly pushed the toy sword through his belt so that he could make one of his best bows to the visitor.

Jordon was delighted. Both with the performance and with the lady's words. "Mistress, I think you have founded a dynasty."

Isabel allowed a slight softness as she looked up at her eldest son, though she could never acknowledge him as such. "Two, I hope." Then she ruffled Tom's hair affectionately, releasing him to fight imaginary brigands out in the yard.

Jordon opened his mouth, trying to think of something to say which would not compromise Mistress Fytton, when the door of an upper room clicked shut and a young woman descended the stair. His mouth stayed open and he stared, not believing what he saw.

"Ah. Benedicta. You remember her, Jordon? Poor Petronilla's daughter. She has taken the place of her mother and has made an excellent maid and I don't know what I would do without her. Benedicta, dear. Would you bestir Tilda and bring Master de Bolyn refreshment."

Jordon watched every movement as the girl with the long, honey-coloured plaits, the large hazelnut eyes, and the full red lips insinuated her slim figure across the width of the hall towards the kitchen. Never had he seen a female so perfectly rounded in just the right places. And never had he felt so foolish when acquainted with his own desires. His member was so erect it ached. And for Benedicta Dane! He couldn't believe it.

"Poor Petronilla?" He made a determined effort to concentrate. "Ah . . . " He remembered. "That unfortunate episode over Banaster. But surely she is over that by now . . . "

"You don't know, then." It was a statement rather than a question. "Of course. You went back to London . . . " Isabel motioned him to the best chair, taking a seat on the high-backed wooden bench to await Benedicta's return. "Petronilla was with child by Banaster when Thomas ... " She hesitated. "When my husband saw fit to remove his head. By the time the child was ready to be born she had lost the will to live, blaming herself for all that had befallen Ralph and finding her shame too much to bear. To have taken her husband's murderer to her bed ... "

"So the child died too." Jordon suddenly found the edge of his shirt sleeve very interesting as he tried not to think of Angareta. If he had stayed with her, it might have been different. But then again, it might not.

"No. Why do you say that?" Isabel noticed his sudden sobriety. As no answer was forthcoming, she continued. "No. The child was a healthy girl, but Petronilla wouldn't even look at her. She turned away and from that moment she neither ate nor drank. Nor said one word to anyone. In two days she breathed her last."

"And the child?" Jordon thought of how the son he never even saw now lay in the churchyard beside the River Thames.

"Elizabeth? She is only a few weeks

older than my Thomas. A boisterous child with fiery curls and a winning smile. She'll break hearts aplenty before she's finished. Christiana took her." Isabel gazed pensively into the middle distance. Christiana, and Geoffrey, and Belle, as she was affectionately known. They seemed so happy. A family. Just as Christiana had always wished. The fact that Bernulf still hadn't married her didn't seem to matter any more.

How the world had changed in so short a time! Isabel and Thomas Fytton, and young Tom, his half-brother. And Bernulf and Christiana with a child they probably thought by now was actually their own. Perhaps he'd call at the cot by the river before he left. No doubt the place itself would be the same. He glanced up as Benedicta returned carrying ale and food. Yes. Things had certainly changed! Mostly for the better!

"To prosperity." Isabel raised her cup to the young man, bringing his attention away from her maid.

"Prosperity." Jordon smiled, a feeling of relaxation coming over him. A feeling of belonging. Of being at home. It was an illusion, he knew, but for the first time in his life he felt that Isabel de Orreby, now Mistress Fytton, was doing all she could to make up for past mistakes. And he was grateful.

"I shall show you the accounts, if you are still interested. I remember how you used to follow Nicholas Bailiff like a shadow when you were a boy. I've increased the flock threefold, thanks to your business and," she leaned forward, smiling, "I don't know whether this will please you or not, but this new-found wealth has made the new Gawsworth Hall a certainty. Bernulf and Francis Miller, his assistant, already have the plans for the foundations."

Jordon whistled under his breath. Then he observed the woman opposite him, his chin resting on his hand, and their eyes met in mutual understanding. There was something about this place. It was more than just a place to live. It wove a spell around all who came under its roof. It claimed them, and once claimed, they could never escape. They found themselves obliged to work towards perpetuating the essence of Gawsworth.

Bernulf had lived with that feeling all his life. It was more than selfish ambition which kept him on the estate. He could have left when he was young and probably made his fortune with the skills he had acquired. He could have left when Isabel turned her back on him for Sir John. And there was even more cause when she married Fytton. But still he stayed. For love of Gawsworth. His ancestral earth. It was in his bones, and just as surely it was in the bones of Jordon de Bolyn. And the bones of Isabel de Orreby. For a split second Jordon had a vision of generations of their descendants making pilgrimages to this acre of land beside the lakes, drawn by an irresistible force to the core of their existence. For a renewal of the spirit and a restoration of the soul. Mayhap his own sons, one day . . . If it hadn't been for Isabel telling him of the new business to be had over at Bechton, where Peter Legh was raising his family, his thoughts would have strayed back to the lithe figure and swaying hips of the girl with the honey-coloured hair. But there was plenty of time for that. If he was to visit Bechton, and the Bernulf cot, and one or two other old haunts, there was plenty of time.

"So, Legh has heard of the money to be made, has he?" The London merchant had that gleam in his eye when he saw new prospects. The same determination he saw in the woman opposite. In the new-found closeness this provided he felt moved to tell her more of his plans. He trusted her, and by the transactions she had conducted recently, he knew she trusted him. "And there may be more for you," he nodded amiably. "I also buy from others. Notably, Hugh de Spenser."

Isabel was suddenly more alert. "De Spenser?" There was more to the question than the trade of wool. She had heard all about Hugh and the King. Was Jordon at the same games he had played with John Grindon?

Well aware of the thoughts going through her mind, Jordon chose to ignore the insinuation. "Aye. He has extensive holdings, and has had the foresight to bring new strains of sheep from across the Channel, resulting in thicker wool. More tons to the flock. Most of these he keeps in Northamptonshire and as we are partners . . . I'm sure I can persuade him to let me send a few to Gawsworth to improve your own."

"Partners?" Isabel raised an eyebrow. What did he mean by partners?

Jordon couldn't keep his face straight any longer. "Business partners." He grinned at the disbelief on her face. "Truly. And not only in wool." He told her of Hugh de Spenser's visit to the house John Grindon had left him, and the deal he had struck. The information provided by the merchant ensured a splendid haul for the pirate every time, and the bounty split to the satisfaction of both. "Much of my share can be disposed of under the guise of legitimate business," Jordon told her. "But on occasion I have been somewhat embarrassed by the magnificence of the goods . . . " He stopped speaking, becoming thoughtful. "The kind of thing that needs to disappear for a while until the true owners despair of finding it. Silver-gilt plate. Large stones, some uncut. Durable things which will not harm in storage . . . "

"In storage . . . " Isabel caught his meaning. There was the tunnel with its secret chamber . . .

"And should the worst befall me, either at the hands of irate customers or in war, then the spoils will be put to good use here. The new hall. The estate." He smiled. Thomas will one day want more than a wooden sword if he is aught like his dam.

"Jordon . . . " There was tragedy in her voice as she said his name. If only . . . He should be the master here. He could build this manor to greater heights than even she dreamed of. If only . . .

"The past shapes our future," he said, touching her hand in understanding. "And had my past been different mayhap I should not have had the courage to go out as I have. Mayhap I would have been content to let the world go by. Like my father."

Isabel sighed, but not unhappily. He was right. They all had to come to terms with reality and not hanker for the moon. Thank God this man had learnt the lesson in his youth. "I think you will do very well." She squeezed the hand which touched her own. And by the look she gave him then he knew she was proud of him. They had made their peace. They were content.

★ ★ ★

Benedicta Dane was in heaven as she walked the length of Spitalgate towards their lodgings in Coxwell Street in the town of Cirencester. Jordon de Bolyn had promised to marry her and they were on their way to his house in London, stopping in this town on the way to conduct business and admire the building work on the Church of St. John the Baptist. His donation had been larger than most and he was sure of a welcome amongst his fellows in trade. To Benedicta it seemed that the world was built in wool! And now, only today, they had heard that King Edward was to hold his Christmas Court at the Abbey. There would be merrymaking such as she had only imagined. Her breath steamed out in front of her in the cold, misty air, her hair was damp and her feet wet through. But she was happy.

So was Jordon. Business was brisk, and that always made him happy. And his honey-haired mistress made him happy. His enjoyment of her was as deep as it was unexpected and he knew that for the first time in his life the emotion in his heart and mind was the thing men called love. He didn't understand it. He only knew that this time it was different. And he never for a moment compared the slightly elfin face of the slender figure or the fascinating hair with that other girl from his past. Alditha Cherry. His first experience of the female sex. He couldn't know that the great merchant of London was still clinging to the one moment of love in his youth.

The other reason for his happiness was the King. Lancaster, it seemed, had held an assembly at Doncaster and issued a document in which King Edward was accused of assisting Hugh de Spenser in his new career, and the King had sent for Jordon.

"This," said the King, "is the excuse I have been waiting for." He was strolling along the winding path beside the River Chum, Jordon de Bolyn by his side and the rest of his followers at a distance enough to render them out of earshot. "He has threatened me with rebellion over this and other matters, even though there could never be proof of my involvement in the piracy charge."

"Your Majesty speaks the truth," Jordon agreed. "There is most definitely no proof." He flexed his fingers inside his gloves to keep the blood flowing. The King seemed not to notice the cold.

"I wish you to be my envoy in this. Archbishop Reynolds shall direct the Convocation to declare de Spenser's exile invalid and Hugh shall come home immediately." Edward noticed the flash of concern on the other man's face and understood it. "However, I recognise that not all are as innocent as myself, and must therefore lose by this change in circumstance. Which is a pity in the light of the service they have done de Spenser. I therefore propose that you accept a position in my household." Edward smiled. "If that is agreeable."

Jordon was dumbfounded. A position in the King's household! It was far more than he expected and certainly made up for the loss in revenue Hugh de Spenser's return would precipitate. He fell onto one knee, there by the small lake in the Abbey grounds, and kissed his King's hand. Like his father before him, he fell under the spell of his monarch, Edward, second of that name.

★ ★ ★

The first bright shafts of morning sunlight shot like lances over the rim of the surrounding hills, touching a snow-softened landscape with the glitter of gold as Isabel crunched her way past the lakes and down towards the village. She hoped the thaw was on its way. It was almost lambing time again. How time seemed to fly! Once Ralph Dane had been the shepherd. Now Jack Sharpe's brother Matthew had taken on the role, having learnt the job over on the Warburton estates towards the west of the country. And there had been other changes instigated by the Lady of the Manor. Timothy Reeve had been replaced by Edgar Baguley, brother of Maud the miller's wife and Maud's daughter,

Tansy, the middle one of the miller's five girls, now did most of the work in the kitchen of the Hall. Tilda hadn't the strength to pluck a goose these days but she had been in charge for so long that it would have been cruel to show her the door. And anyway, there was a wealth of information in that old head to be passed on to the next generation of cooks. Isabel knew she had every right to be pleased with herself. Her husband could indulge himself in politics and fighting for ever for all she cared. The more he went on his travels in search of mischief, the more she enjoyed life. There was no love between them, nor ever would be. The woman, muffled in squirrel and marten, listened to the stillness of the morning, its silence broken only by her crisp footsteps on the crust of the frozen snow. Her face glowed with a health sustained by hard work and determination, though the once seductive mouth rarely smiled these days. The happiness was all inside. Protected by a hard and inflexible shell of authority. She would never be hurt again as long as she lived. How could she be when the only thing she loved was this estate?

These woods and hills and lakes and rivers. This Hall. She had no time for other loves. No time at all.

The earth and timber barns beside Nicholas Bailiff's office were in sight when she saw the band of men emerge from the path through Three Mile Wood and Isabel slowed her pace. Yesterday she had watched as Thomas Fytton had ridden away to war on his mighty Cheshire steed, bred specially to carry a man encased in the weight of chain-mail. He had looked magnificent in the blue and silver tabard, carrying a shield emblazoned with three garbs d'or as he raised his sword in a farewell salute to young Tom. He was a more powerful man, physically, than either of his brothers and they had appeared weak beside him. Unlike Robert Holland, the Earl of Lancaster's favourite household knight since the day he had presented him with the head of Adam Banaster. He too had muscle, and was not afraid to use it. They had taken with them a company of men. Archers and lancers. But some familiar faces had been missing. Tom Helesby, Dickon Miller, and his young brother, Francis. None of the many Sharpe boys, nor any member of the Baguley family. But most notably, Geoffrey Bernulf. And now, in the brilliance of the morning, Isabel knew why. They were marching to fight under the King's colours. Thomas Fytton was for Lancaster and the Earls. Half closing her eyes against the brightness the Lady of Gawsworth drew a sharp breath of cold air. A rider had appeared over the horizon, cantering down the snowy tracts towards the men, his head high and bearing almost regal. Jordon de Bolyn had arrived to lead the contingent of Cheshire men to the King in the north-east of the country where the battle for the crown of England was destined to take place. And beside him, equally proud, equally brave, strode the greatest archer of them all. Bernulf. The young man's father. The peasant who had spoken not a single word to the Lady since the night of Banaster's execution, except in cases of necessity. And then he had doffed his cap without looking her in the face, and touched his forelock with his head bowed. He had never forgiven her.

Isabel took an involuntary step forward, her hand stretched towards the disappearing men. Her heart beat against her ribs in painful rhythm and her head buzzed with fear. Civil War! Jordon de Bolyn and Geoffrey Bernulf against Thomas, John and Hugh Fytton. Lancaster against his King. Isabel turned. Nicholas Bailiff could wait. With her thoughts in turmoil she made her way back, not to the house, but to the tiny and somewhat poorly maintained church beside the Hall, and there she fell to her knees on the cold stone floor and tried to pray. But the words would not come. She knew not what to pray for. And for all the furs and velvets she wore, the chill within her breast remained, and her heart seemed to turn to ice.

★ ★ ★

King Edward and his knights were in a spirited frame of mind as they rested after a day's march north. The campaign against the Marcher Lords had been both bloodless and victorious and though Hereford, Damory and Mowbray had fled north to Lancaster's army, Audley *and* the Mortimers had surrendered and had been duly imprisoned.

"Your Majesty." Jordon bowed to the King. He knew that Edward was almost ready to attend Mass and should be acquainted with the news immediately. "Sir Andrew Harclay seeks audience. It seems that the Bruce has been devastating the far north . . . "

"Robert Bruce is the last of my worries tonight," Edward muttered. Still, if Harclay has marched from Carlisle, he'd better see him.

"Devastated!" Sir Andrew could not stress the fact enough. "Raid after raid. And Lancaster standing by towards the east without raising a finger in defence of our lands . . . "

"And there you have it," Edward thundered. "Lancaster! He has been the thorn in my side for too long, and by God I shall remove him before he poisons me completely! Forget Bruce until the nonce. We advance on Pontefract. And you, Sir Andrew, can go further. North of York might be an advantage for, if it is as you say and Lancaster has allowed the Scots to rampage within a gobspit of his own lands, it is not beyond possibility that he has reached even more certain agreement with them. Cut him off from his allies. We shall have him like a flea between finger and thumb!"

Outside the tents, in the bitter cold of a February night, men huddled round fires, making stews out of salted meat and turnip and discussing the state of their world as they ate.

"Robert Lewer rides with us, then." Tom Helesby licked the inside of his bowl to clean it.

"But for how long?" Dickon Miller wondered. "He's had Odiham returned to him, but he's always looking over the fence to see if the grass is greener. It's fine whilst he's with us though. The murdering bastard!" Dickon spat into the fire.

"As are Swynnerton and Middleton. And they are with us too," Tom remarked. "Lancaster doesn't stand a chance!"

"Nothing's certain," Geoffrey Bernulf couldn't help reminding them. "Lancaster has the likes of Gurney and Ogle, neither of them milksops. And what about Maltravers and Thomas de Berkley? Have you seen them today? Hesketh? Or his man Simon Barford?"

The rest of the Cheshire archers fell silent, none of them wishing to come across any of those named in a confrontation. It was better to have such men at your elbow fighting a common enemy. No one was looking forward to it. What if they came face to face with Thomas Fytton? Their legal master? Would they injure him? Always supposing he didn't see them into the next world before they could realise it. It didn't bear thinking about. But fight they would if fight they must. And they would follow Jordon de Bolyn proudly in the King's just and legitimate cause. Which is why, when the order came the following morning, they could be seen marching briskly north in company with the men of Cumberland and Westmorland under the flag of Sir Andrew Harclay whose sole intention was to get the skirmish over with so that the enemy across the border could be dealt with.

On the morning of March 16th, 1322,

Sir Andrew Harclay drew his army up in the formation of schiltroms, their spears thrust upwards and outwards to form impenetrable walls. On both flanks they were supported by archers. No one could cross the River Ure by the bridge at Boroughbridge without a tremendous fight, and Lancaster, having seen the sparkle of metal across the great flat expanse of snow-drifted landscape, decided to divide his forces. Hereford and Clifford he placed in charge of the infantry, taking the cavalry himself, intending to cross the river at a nearby ford. Hereford advanced towards the bridge and the Cheshire archers fitted arrows to their bows.

"Where's Jordon?" Dickon squinted against sun reflected off snow.

"He went down to the bridge with those Welshmen," Geoffrey answered. "Though if they're left without a commander in the fray they'll no doubt turn tail again and run. We'll answer to Harclay at the call anyway." The archers had their weapons trained towards the ford and Lancaster's cavalry.

As the first horse entered the water,

they fired and rearmed. Their aim was true and a number of the cavalry fell, the screaming horses thrashing out their death throes in the icy water, blocking the ford for those following as they did so. The second flurry of arrows was just as successful, and the third. It was then that they saw those in the middle of the melee try to turn from the deadly storm of sharpened steel. They had won. For the moment.

At the bridge, Jordon de Bolyn helped place the infantry to best advantage. The bridge itself was not in good repair and as he stood under it he could see daylight through the rotten planking above. *He* had a thought. It was worth a try and would only need a couple of men.

"Here! You." He called a Welshman to him. "How well do you wield that spear?" The man approached him, grinning wide enough to show the blackened stumps of his remaining teeth. There was no need to ask one of Gruffyd Lloyd's men a question like that! He stood beside the Englishman and looked up to see what he had in mind.

"Could you spear a man through the

crack?" Jordon poked at the soft wood with his sword, widening the hole. "Just one or two brought down so unexpectedly would start a panic."

It was at that moment that Hereford decided to lead his men into battle. Literally. He was at their head and first onto the bridge with a roar of encouragement.

The Welshman weighed his weapon in his right hand and poised his body, taut and still. His ears strained for every footstep. His eye watched for the merest shadow above his head. The shadow of the enemy. Then his arm straightened in a massive thrust, his aim accurate to a hair's breadth. The deafening screech of agony as Hereford was castrated before the spear entered the soft part of his belly stung their ears. With a powerful pull the soldier retrieved his weapon, pulling the body down onto the wood of the bridge above them. Jordon was not quick enough. Blood gushed between the planking and covered him before he could mount his horse to take part in the battle. When he finally emerged, he posed such a demonic sight that none of the enemy took what was to be their best chance of finishing him and when his own men caught sight of him they at first feared he had been mortally wounded. A cheer went up when they realised the truth.

Lancaster, on seeing the heavy losses on the bridge and the depletion of his own force, withdrew. Many of his men were dead. Some were taken prisoner in case hostages should be required. And the rest had lost some of their enthusiasm.

It was another bitterly cold night and the men had slept little, thoughts of further battle keeping dreams at bay, but with the morning sun came an unexpected warmth to thaw the winter snow enough to show that spring was not too far away. It cheered them. As did the sight which greeted their eyes. Having witnessed the horrific end of their leader, most of Hereford's men had deserted during the night and now stood on the King's side of the river. What was more, after the capture of Thomas Fytton of Gawsworth by none other than Hugh de Spenser himself, Lancaster's chief lieutenant, Robert Holland had also defected under cover of dark. The battle was over before another shot had been fired. Lancaster faced defeat with the rising sun on the seventeenth day of March.

Geoffrey Bernulf stood outside Pontefract Castle knowing that he was growing old. He had seen it all before, except that the last time it had been Gaveston they led out. And the castle had been Warwick. And the day had been in the heat of June. But the sentence was the same. Death by beheading. Ten years ago, all but three months. He allowed a cynical smile. Lancaster, having then played the part of executioner, now took on the role of victim, and Geoffrey Bernulf, then holding Gaveston's ruby in his hand had thought his dreams fulfilled. He had been even more of a fool than the man who knelt before the block, his hair covered by the black linen cap and his eyes blindfolded. He had only wanted the crown. Geoffrey had wanted more. He had wanted Isabel, Lady of Gawsworth. He cleared his throat loudly and spat into the slush. That one jewel made him a rich man, yet he had left it in its hiding place in the tunnel. It was not what he wanted. Not in itself. There was nothing he wanted now. Not since the woman had shown herself in her true colours and made him realise just how much of an idiot he had been over the years.

The townspeople had jeered and pelted the earl with cold, melting snow, ridiculing the man they had only lately shown deference to as their lord. Then the axe was raised. It whistled through the air at speed but the head was only partly severed. A blood-lust roar shattered the silence and the axe fell again. This time the head rolled free. Gaveston was avenged.

The archer turned away with a shrug. All men had their problems and he was no different from most, but at least he still had his head. He was stopped by a hand on his arm.

"Father." Jordon had been searching the crowds for him. "You led the men in the field magnificently and when I mentioned it to the King he insisted that he renews your acquaintance. And you saved my skin. Granted I saw Hereford off, but I should have been attacking Lancaster at the ford at the time, and had you not had the experience . . . "

Geoffrey grinned at his son. "What else should I have done? Twiddled my thumbs until you decided to turn up? Let Lancaster trample those young lads from Gawsworth?"

"Come then," Jordon tugged at his arm. "The King waits . . . and what could he have meant by . . . what did he say? Thatching! On a rooftop in Macclesfield? Something about a promise . . . "

That same afternoon Jordon de Bolyn, member of the King's household, was astounded by King Edward's words.

" . . . and for the services of both father and son, and in consequence of the promise once made, I hereby grant the Manor and lands known as Gawsworth in seisin to Jordon de Bolyn for his lifetime and thereafter to his named successor, asking only that he use the Lady Isabel of Gawsworth well for the hospitality she has shown us."

Thomas Fytton, languishing with his comrade in arms Robert Holland at his

Majesty's pleasure in the Tower, had lost his lands to the man his nephews had once made cruel fun of. And for all the world cared he might just as well have forfeited his life.

8

THE irony of it brought a sardonic smile to the sweat-streaked face of Geoffrey Bernulf. The new Gawsworth Hall was being built on the very spot where the old Bernulf cot had stood in the days before the Norman lords had marched the length of England sharing out the spoils amongst themselves. And his grandsire's grandsire, Bernulf the freeman, would be well pleased at the way events had turned out. A great Hall to replace his cot, and his descendant Jordon de Bolyn the master of the estate. Geoffrey had once wished that this might be so, but with never a hope that wishes on stars ever came true.

"Ahh ... " Francis Miller stopped digging as he caught sight of a movement up at the house. Then he gave a low whistle. "If that isn't a sight to gladden a man's eyes ... "

"Food! I'm so hungry I could eat even

Tansy's burnt offerings." Piers Baguley rubbed his stomach and licked his lips.

"So could I!" Will Sharpe was quick to agree. The lad had taken his father's place at Gawsworth since Jack had left to set up house with Alditha Cherry, at Lane Ends. Will liked the arrangement. It was better at Gawsworth. At Lane Ends his mother was always sending him on long messages in all weathers, to keep him out of her way. And she'd only allowed his father Jack to live with her on condition he became a woodsman, and woodsmen were away for days at a time.

"Hey! That's my niece you are maligning." Francis stung their ears with a quick slap apiece. Though he had to agree that Dickon's daughter was taking her time in reaching Tilda's standards. But it was neither the food nor Tansy Miller that had caused him to whistle. His niece was accompanied by Mistress Isabel's new maid, Martha Davenport. Will Davenport's younger sister. Benedicta Dane's replacement.

"And so the world goes round," Geoffrey Bernulf chuckled, watching his assistant drooling over the fourteen-year-old, with her untroubled smile and innocent eyes. It wasn't two minutes ago that he had proffered an invitation to the girl's mistress. Or so it seemed. And look at the trouble that had landed him in! "Have sense, lad. Leave well alone!"

Francis looked at the older man as though he were mad. But then, what could a man of Bernulf's years know of love? He could never have felt pounding of the heart or the rushing of the blood. Or the aching member trying to embarrass its owner. These were things only young men knew of.

Piers and Will had run towards the girls as they approached, peeping under the cloths to see what manner of food they had brought and poking their fingers into the baskets to steal a morsel or two. Geoffrey wiped his forehead on the back of his arm and rubbed some of the dirt from his hands in readiness. As he did so he saw them. Christiana's limp was so pronounced these days that it almost looked as though she were dipping in a curtsey every time she put her weight on her left foot. But her hair still glinted gold, as it had when she was twelve years old. And her skin showed no sign of a wrinkle or a hint of advancing years. Skipping alongside her was the wiry little girl he had come to think of as his daughter. Elizabeth. His Belle. With her fiery locks and freckled face she had enough personality for a dozen children. They too had a basket which he knew would contain more food, and probably fresh herbs for Christiana's potions and cures. He made his way down to the bridge across the lake to meet them.

"We were gathering in Three Mile Wood," Christiana smiled. "So we thought we would join you for a bite to eat."

Geoffrey slipped his arm around her waist and gave her a squeeze. There had never been that all-consuming passion between them, but the woman had loved him since . . . He hugged her again. He couldn't remember a time when she hadn't been there, looking after him. Perhaps he should have married her . . . but there was always something . . . Something elusive and indefinable, holding him back from that final, irrevocable step. Even now, he couldn't do it. Despite everything.

Up at the Hall, Isabel Fytton had been humming a tune the wandering minstrel had played the week before. The accounts were healthy and in order and she was busy composing a letter to send to Jordon about the next consignment. Everything had worked out so well. Thanks to her son's business skill and bravery in battle, he had not only become wealthy, but the master of Gawsworth too. Some things, she thought, were simply meant to be. And the new Hall was beginning to take shape, the oak spars already cut and the foundations almost laid. There was to be a kerridge floor. Stone. Not bare earth as in this hall. Maybe even a kerridge roof. Bernulf had been finding new skills in the cutting of the stone from the quarry ... She strolled to the window-slit to look down the slope to the old stable yard where the building was going on. It was then that she saw them. Geoffrey with his arm around Christiana and young Belle tugging at his hand. How complete they looked. How much the happy family. A familiar lump rose in her throat.

"What is it, Mother?" Tom had been

trying to help her with the accounts, but it was a pastime which soon had him bored.

"Oh, nothing. Only the girls taking the builders their food." She turned away, not wanting to see.

Tom peered through the opening, straining on tip-toe to look over the high sill. At ten years of age he was growing fast, but not fast enough for his own liking. "Oh! It's her! I bet she'd rather go fishing than sit with the builders. She's good at fishing you know. For a girl!"

Then he was off, galloping like a horse and slapping his thigh as he went. Isabel couldn't help laughing. She spoilt the boy, she knew. But he was so wonderfully open. Completely without guile or cunning. And she couldn't help loving him far more than was good for her, but she needed someone to love. And her husband still languished in the Tower, forgotten, it seemed, by everyone.

Down in the old stableyard it took only a moment for Tom to persuade Belle that it was an ideal day for fishing.

"Please, please, please, Father." She entwined her warm slender arms around Geoffrey's neck and kissed his rough cheek.

Much as he hated the thought of her spending her time with Fytton's lad, he could not refuse her, and as he watched the children run down to the water's edge he reached for Christiana's hand. She squeezed his fingers sympathetically. "Whatever will be, will be," she whispered.

He could only agree.

* * *

"I don't know what the world is coming to," Benedicta grumbled. "A whole groat for a roast hen!" There was plenty of money in the pocket tied to her girdle; silver groats, pennies and farthings. But she had not been brought up to waste money and it was hard for her to change. Unlike the world she lived in.

"Then take three pigeons. Only tuppence-ha'penny," the red-faced poulterer told her. He'd had a hard day and couldn't be bothered to haggle. "And unless I'm much mistaken, you'll be wishing for these prices in a few weeks from now. When Queen Isabella invades England with her fancy-man! There'll be little enough to sell, let alone bargain over."

The streets of London were buzzing with rumour and gossip. By all accounts, letters had been speeding across the Channel between the English and French Courts by the minute. The rot had really set in a couple of years previously when Mortimer of Wigmore had managed to escape from the Tower of London by getting his guards drunk and descending from his window via a rope. Jordon de Bolyn had been incensed at the time, the men thought to have aided Mortimer being none other than his colleagues Richard de Bettoyne and John de Gisors. And they were not alone in adhering to the Queen's cause. Hugh de Spenser had trodden on many toes since the death of Lancaster and the executed earl was now almost venerated as a saint. Consequently, King Edward had a growing army of malcontents ranged against him, a situation only made worse by Edmund of Woodstock, Earl of Kent, who had turned a diplomatic incident in France into almost all-out war. Kent then turned to the Queen. As did the Bishops of Winchester and Norwich, the Earls of Richmond and Leicester, and even Edward's old friend Sir Henry de Beaumont.

Jordon was late home as usual and Benedicta waited impatiently. She was determined to know the truth. Could the poulterer possibly be right? Was there about to be a dearth of pullet and pigeon? Not to mention sole and eels and flounder! When men were called to war bellies were left less than full! Ah! She heard the rattle of the latch and the scraping of his shoes on the slop-stone. The streets didn't get any cleaner, despite the new laws against throwing waste through front doors and windows. And it wasn't just the people. It was their animals too. Dogs and cats and pigs and chickens. All seemed to have right of way beyond the house door.

"Roast pigeon." Benedicta bustled about removing her husband's coat and bringing his house shoes. "The hens were a groat each and I accused the fellow of robbing his customers. And what did he say? That I'd be willing to pay his price soon, if I could still get it, because there is to be a war." The woman pulled up a stool to the table as Jordon cut into the first of the birds with his dagger. "Tell me, Husband. Is that so? Will Queen Isabella bring an army from France to fight her husband?"

Jordon wiped a dribble of gravy from his chin and chewed on the tender flesh for a moment before answering. For all she was only a meddlesome woman, he was surprised to find that he was still in love with his wife. The long, honey-coloured hair was now securely hidden under her coif, as befitted a good wife, and her clothes were plainer and less seductive than previously. But still he loved her. "There is fresh news," he told her. "Isabella has gone beyond the bounds of decency with Mortimer and hops brazenly into his bed at every opportunity. So much so that even her brother cannot condone her behaviour and she has now travelled to the Court of the Count of Aquitaine with

Prince Edward, proposing that her son marries the Count's daughter Philippa." He paused to break open the second pigeon. "Which means that she will be petitioning for the dowry so that she can raise an army."

"So there will be a war." Benedicta picked forlornly at a broken nail. The price of poultry could be double!

"The trouble is . . . " Jordon spoke almost to himself. He thought of Hugh de Spenser's growing unpopularity. "The trouble is that not everyone has had the good fortune to see eye to eye with de Spenser. He has the King's ear and there are many who are jealous both of his power and his wealth. But since he altered trade conditions and improved the possibilities of even greater profits for those quick enough to take advantage of the change, I think some of the blame can be laid at their own doors. They expect life to be handed to them on a platter . . ."

Benedicta hid a smile. He was off on one of his tirades. "But what about the war? When will the invasion begin?"

"Who knows?" Jordon belched and

stretched his shoulders in the way he always did. "Tomorrow. Next week. Next month." He felt replete. Comfortable. In his own home. With his own wife. "Come here, Mistress." He held out his arms to her. Should he take her to bed? Or should he risk Hodge or Mary, her maid, bursting in on them? He picked at the ties on her dress and the prim and proper face she showed to the world dissolved in a cascade of girlish giggles. Why worry about a war that might never happen!

★ ★ ★

When it happened it happened overnight. King Edward offered a reward for Mortimer's head, and the Archbishop of Canterbury issued a papal bill against invaders, this time from across the Channel rather than from across the northern borders. It made not the slightest difference. Isabella and her army landed in Suffolk before the end of September, and Mortimer was at her side. And as they marched towards London those who had reason to hate Hugh de Spenser flocked to join her.

King Edward, inside the fortified Tower, felt the growing hostility of the capital and escaped its confines before it became a prison guarded by the people. And as he fled west towards Wales in the company of a handful of friends including de Spenser, Arundel and Surrey, London declared for the Queen.

"Come, Wife! Take only as much as you can carry and my men will arrive shortly to bring the rest. And you, Hodge . . . " Jordon turned to his servant, "Look after Mary. We are taking her with us." He looked about him distractedly. "The best plate. And the two salvers . . . Thank God I sent so much up to Gawsworth previously . . . Ah!" He sighed with relief as four swarthy men strode in through the door.

Within minutes the household was on the move, through the Chepe and down towards the river. There a small trading ship awaited them and by hurrying them aboard, herding them like a flock of sheep, Jordon made sure that they sailed on the tide. And less than two weeks later the *Sparrowhawk* tied up at Chester, unloading its cargo of people, goods and chattels onto the sandstone quay.

"More serious than the struggle with Lancaster?" Isabel frowned at her son and his wife. They had finished Tansy's somewhat inelegant meal and were trying to quench the after-taste with ale. The party from London had arrived at Gawsworth rather unexpectedly.

"Oh . . . " Benedicta wrung her hands. The things she had witnessed as they fled would be with her till she died.

Jordon patted her shoulder soothingly. "As we made our way through the streets we came upon a mob led by Robert Lewer, baying for the blood of Hugh de Spenser." He closed his eyes and swallowed. "Unfortunately, it was not Hugh in the street, but his servant, John le Marshal. A very good friend of mine. There was nothing we could have done to help him. They were screaming like the hordes from Hell and the next thing we knew, we were paddling in his blood as it ran down the gutter."

Isabel gasped. "London has gone mad!"

"That wasn't all," Jordon continued. "As we crossed we were witness to an even worse atrocity. Bishop Stapleton was in full flight, his robes billowing out behind him across the square as he tried to reach the sanctuary of St Paul's. But they caught him before he reached the steps." Jordon put his head in his hands as he relived the moment. "They used a butcher's knife. And hacked his head from his body."

"And is the King safe?" Isabel could not bear to contemplate rule under Queen Isabella. Not with Mortimer at her side.

"Fled. But we shall find him. He will need help." Jordon stood and strode briskly round the hall as he thought. "You will take care of my wife for me until I return. And I shall need men. Not many at first, until we see the way things are. Just one or two of the best. The ones we can trust with our lives."

"Bernulf . . . " Isabel knew that Geoffrey would never betray his son. Not for all the jewels in the King's crown.

* * *

If Edward was to find friends anywhere then it was in Wales, the land of his birth, where many of the estates in the south of the country had long been in the hands of Hugh de Spenser. Cautiously they moved from manor to manor, keeping one step ahead of the enemy. They heard that Isabella and her paramour had entered Bristol on the surrender of the Earl of Winchester. For all that he refused to fight, he received no mercy and was executed as a traitor, Norfolk, Leicester and Kent assisting Mortimer to arrive at the judgement.

In Glamorgan, de Spenser ordered his tenants to arm in the King's cause, only to find refusal at every turn. One disgruntled servant decided to take matters into his own hands and, waiting until the end of Sunday service, approached the minister in the guise of a penitent, confessing to Rhys ap Howel the whereabouts of the fugitives. That day Henry of Lancaster captured not only de Spenser but King Edward and his chancellor Robert Baldock too.

Jordon de Bolyn lost the race to find the King and Isabella and Mortimer waited at Hereford for the arrival of the prisoners. It was there that Hugh de Spenser was tried and found guilty of a long list of charges, some fact, but most pure fiction.

Fallen autumn leaves were wet and rotting in the late November chill, filling the air with the scent of decay and despondency as Hugh de Spenser was led out to suffer in public. A platform, hastily erected on four barrels borrowed from the cooper, gave an eager audience the chance to view the whole proceedings, and by the joyous numbers milling about the area there was little doubt that Queen Isabella had won the day.

As Jordon watched Hugh's face, impassive and staring at distant horizons, he felt his own bowels bubble and churn and an icy sweat dampen his shirt. "There, but by the grace of God, go I." The linen shirt on Jordon's back was covered with a rough wool smock borrowed from Hodge Pearson, and he stood barefoot with the rest of the peasants. Ostentation would serve nothing today. Witness Hugh de Spenser! *He* had developed the trade of England more efficiently in a few short years than could have been achieved in a lifetime by any other. He had made good the coin of the realm, and by his part in the drawing up of laws and ordinances had sought to make the land a less difficult place to dwell in. *He* had achieved great heights and seen no virtue in modesty. Until today.

"Whatever happens," Geoffrey muttered under his breath to his son, "we must not have the King brought to this pass whilst there is still breath in our bodies. Rumour has it that the Queen is now in possession of the King's seal and that he is secured in the castle at Kenilworth . . . "

Jordon clenched his fists as a cheer went up from the crowd. Hugh de Spenser had been stripped and now stood before them as naked as the day he was born, the usual wayward lock of hair across his brow. The courtier lifted his hand to push it back with the same casual nonchalance he had always affected, as though today were merely another day. In a split second that pretence vanished as two burly men-at-arms took hold of him, throwing him roughly onto a trestle table, face up and spread-eagled. With cold-blooded precision, his private parts were sliced from his body and held aloft before being thrown onto the waiting fire. The screams, echoing across the River Wye and around Bishop's Meadow were neither those of an arrogant courtier, nor those of a wealthy, ambitious statesman. They were the screams of a defenceless human being.

"So we treat heretics and sodomites!" the sergeant bellowed. "Even those who have knowledge of the King!"

The crowd went wild and Jordon turned away. What was there to be gained by watching more? Disembowelling was not a pastime he found pleasure in.

"I agree." Geoffrey pushed a path through the men and women beside the city walls. "Before the She-Wolf of France continues her desecration elsewhere, we'll make for Kenilworth at first light and see what can be done."

As it transpired, there was nothing to be done, but the King was apparently in reasonable health, though much given to wondering where he had gone wrong to alienate his people to such an extent that they hated him. In his youth, when he had left government resting on other shoulders, they had accused him of frivolity and shallowness and made his dear friend Gaveston a scapegoat. In his maturity, when he had bested the man who had for years tried to usurp the crown, he was betrayed. By his own wife! How did he deserve such treachery? He would never understand. Perhaps he had been over-generous to his friends, but they had helped him govern, and been at his right hand through thick and thin . . . Other men's jealousy had been his downfall. And now he doubted he had any friends left . . . It was, he thought, his darkest hour. In that he was wrong.

"And well met!" Jordon de Bolyn slapped the new arrival on the back. Wind was howling under the thatch at the Primrose Inn in the village and anyone with sense was within spitting distance of the central fire in the most hospitable establishment for miles.

"By Satan's breath! You're down on your luck!" Simon Barford pulled at the rough-wool smock, now stinking through constant wear. "What brings our good merchant so far from his prosperity?"

"There are many things not as they

were," Jordon grinned. "I could ask the same of you."

"Let's drink." Geoffrey found ale the best thing to loosen a man's tongue, and he felt that Simon had news for them.

"Hesketh's come with the deputation," Simon began, sliding the scum from the ale with his thumb before drinking. "And Trussell's the spokesman."

Lancaster's men in the past! Jordon and his father leaned forward. It didn't sound good.

"Deputation to what purpose?" Jordon asked.

"Abdication." Simon whispered the word, fearful of being overheard.

The two Cheshire men exchanged a glance. Was Simon Barford for the King? Or for his Lancashire masters? By the way he lowered his voice and looked over his shoulder furtively, they realised there might be a hope. There were those who only pretended to support the Queen in order to stay alive.

"In favour of Prince Edward . . . " He finished yet another cup of ale, trying to put the rest of the tale from his mind.

"And . . . " Simon turned a bleary

eye on Bernulf. The ale and the heat from the fire had done the trick. "And . . . there are those who plot . . . " He coughed as a gust of wind made an entrance and blew fire-smoke in his face. "With cunning. You will see. First the King will be made to feel secure. But then . . ."

His companions waited, knowing he would continue in his own time.

"Maltravers. And his brother-in-law, Berkeley. In Berkeley Castle." Barford gazed moodily into the glowing embers of the part-burnt logs, a plume of spiralling smoke seeming to have a hypnotic effect on his mind. When he spoke again it was as if he were asleep. "Murder," he murmured. "The foulest murder . . ." Simon shuddered despite the almost claustrophobic heat of the crowded inn. "With never a mark to reveal the crime. Unless, as Orleton says, the corpse is put to use by another sodomite . . ." The man started from the horror of his imagination to recognise the concern in the faces of the men he spoke to. "They cannot . . . can they? The King does not deserve such an evil end . . ." Then he retched and spewed sour ale into the already stinking rushes on the floor.

★ ★ ★

Isabel clutched at the edge of the oak board as she recognised the voice of her villein ordering young Will Sharpe to see to his horse. It had been months, and never a word to show whether they were alive or dead! At the top of the stair Benedicta gasped and placed her arms protectively around her swollen belly, her eyes, red through lack of sleep, starting from her head.

"Pray God he still lives!" The young woman sat down on the topmost tread, fearful of falling should the news be bad. Conditions were as insecure now as they had been in the days when Lancaster opposed the King. No one could tell friend from foe, and the people walked in fear.

As Geoffrey Bernulf strode in to confront his Mistress, Isabel noted that though his back was as straight as ever there were subtle streaks of silver glinting in his black hair. She knew that if this man was prepared to speak to her face to face, then the news was not good. Why else would he put aside his grievances? For the first time in twelve years she found herself looking directly into the dark brooding eyes of the man she had never ceased to love.

"Mistress." He refused to acknowledge the softening he saw in her face or the dampness of her lashes. "Jordon sends his respects to yourself and to Mistress Benedicta, his wife." Geoffrey lifted his gaze to the woman still crouched above them on the stairs. "He is well."

At that Benedicta began to weep softly, finding the strength to descend into the hall. "Why has he not come then? Where is he? Not imprisoned?"

Geoffrey noticed her condition. "No, Mistress. But he plans a dangerous mission. To rescue the King from the men who would murder him."

He told them the full facts over a dish of Tansy Miller's stew, a speciality she found almost impossible to spoil. "Orleton forced the King to abdicate in favour of the Prince who has since been crowned the new King of England.

The true King is still a prisoner, but they only await their chance to see him into the next world." He could see that the women found this hard to believe. "But there is hope! Barford, who arrived with the deputation, has no stomach for the plan and was willing to be our man within the castle, and in the event this was a simple matter to arrange. The men set to guard the King are Thomas Gurney and Will Ogle, men known to us this many a year as comrades in arms on the battlefield, though we never quite knew whether they were for us or against us!" He laughed. "Which is how we knew that they always search for the greenest grass!" He looked at Isabel meaningfully. "They can be persuaded . . . At a price!"

Isabel's frown suddenly cleared. "Jordon's plate and jewels!" Stored in the tunnel for safe keeping. But her hands trembled as she thought of the danger. Of the enemy. Of Hugh de Spenser's death . . . Queen Isabella was a woman in love. And a woman in love will go to any lengths . . .

"I see you grow weak at the cost of

loyalty . . . " His voice held the contempt of a hardened soldier.

"Weak?" She felt her face flush with anger. "Fearful for the lives of those I love! But never weak! I'd sooner die myself . . . "

"Good." He was abrupt. "Because Jordon asks that you ride to Chester where the *Sparrowhawk* awaits at anchor. The captain and crew are paid, but likely to have grown lazy after so long in port. You are to instruct them to be ready to sail at short notice. The ship must be provisioned and in trim . . . There are goldsmiths in the port who will buy from you. Take Edgar Baguley for protection." The archer turned away, his mission completed.

Isabel's back was stiff with annoyance and her head held high. But there was nothing she could do or say to change his attitude towards her. Now, or ever. "Tell Jordon it is done." And she left him to prepare for the journey.

On the twenty-third day of September 1327, the *Sparrowhawk*, light on cargo and high in the water, bobbed unnoticed out of the port of Chester and onto the choppy surface of the open sea. The crew scuttled about their business, laughing and cursing and glad to be once more in their natural habitat. Only one man remained quiet and still, gazing back at the land they were leaving.

A brisk wind bellowed the rough brown of the monk's cowl revealing a brief glimpse of unkempt fair hair as it whipped against newly-shaven skin. It snatched a tear from the brimming blue eyes. Perhaps the people were right. Perhaps he was a foundling smuggled into the Queen's bedroom at Caernarfon all those years ago. How much better could a man such as Jordon de Bolyn have ruled England! And how much happier the King of England would have been had he been born a thatcher's son. Edward smiled grimly to himself. God sometimes played malicious jokes on his children. And what would history tell of him? That he loved too deeply? That he tried to better the lot of the peasant in the field? Or simply that he failed. Men being men, he knew it would be that. And he *had* failed. He couldn't deny it.

"God bless you, Geoffrey Bernulf. And

God bless your son!" He shouted into the wind and the words were carried away to the four corners of the earth. "And God have mercy on us," he murmured. There was no response. But perhaps one day, in a small cell on a hillside in Italy, God would speak to him. One day, when he had worn the rock into hollows with his knees and taken the ridges from his fingers telling his beads. And with that thought, Edward, sometime King of England, turned to face distant horizons.

★ ★ ★

Geoffrey Bernulf breathed deeply of the late September air, his skin shivering with remembered fears of that awful night. With the help of Gurney and Ogle they had freed the King, only to be apprehended by a porter. Simon Barford had reacted with the speed of a lightning barb, darting behind the man to kill him crudely but effectively with a single sword-thrust up his arse. And so Edward had made good his escape, leaving his one-time guards, well paid, to present the porter as his dead self and the rumour soon spread that the manner of his dying had been something of poetic justice considering his friendships with Gaveston and de Spenser, amongst many. The people were only too ready to believe such a monstrous tale. Bernulf chuckled to himself. They preferred it to the truth. What excitement was there in knowing that King Edward thanks to Jordon's trading ship, the *Sparrowhawk*, lived in quiet solitude in Italy, contemplating the simple life of ordinary men?

And now summer was almost over. He had just emerged from the tunnel his father had begun all those years ago. It had claimed the old man's life. And now the new Gawsworth was taking shape, though he himself would not live to see it completed. He felt the roughness of the ruby in the palm of his hand and walked slowly to where the kerridge hearthstones had already been laid, not in the centre of the hall this time, but against the wall, with a funnel planned to carry the smoke up through the roof. It promised to be the finest dwelling in the county. Gazing up the slope to the old Gawsworth he felt the familiar tug of his heartstrings and his feet turned in its direction of their own accord. He looked once more as the dying rays of the sun turned the jewel in his hand into a thing of living flame as he walked to stand for the last time under the old oak beside the house, feeling its presence. Its joy. And the way things might have been. Then he walked away.

From the window of her solar, Isabel watched him. He didn't lean against the oak. He just stood there. Thin and gaunt, his clothes hanging from his shoulders as though the flesh had melted away. His cheeks were sunken and his skin waxen. Like the dead. As the thought went through her mind she shook herself. No. It couldn't be. It was a trick of the light. And when she looked again, he had gone.

It was just about a month later that Jordon arrived with his wife and son to stay for the festive season and, as he always did, rode the three miles to the cot on the banks of the River Bolyn. Inside the tiny dwelling Christiana wiped the clammy brow and lifted a dish of soothing tisane to Geoffrey Bernulf's parched lips. The skin was stretched across the bones of his face so tightly that it seemed transparent, and his eyes, always dark, were now sunk into his head and quite without the brooding spark of anger his friends had come to recognise.

"Father." Jordon sank to his knees beside the wool-filled sacks on which the dying man lay. Christiana backed away, stepping outside for a moment to clear her head of the sickly fumes.

"Jordon. My son." Geoffrey lifted a hand, too weak to do more. But in that one small gesture was all the love and pride the older man had always felt but had not been able to speak of. And now it was almost too late. "Bring her. I must make my peace."

A tear stung the great merchant's eye. This man, his father, had dreamed so much, and worked so hard. And yet here he was, dying in the cot he had been born in. His life had been rich in friends and he had fought bravely for his King and country time and time again, being instrumental in the defeat of Lancaster at Boroughbridge. With his help the King had escaped a terrible death. Christiana had loved and cared for him year in, year out, always hoping . . . But the one thing he so desperately desired had eluded him. And now he asked for her. Even at the last, she was his only thought.

As Isabel entered the shadowed room, scented with herbs and woodsmoke and mortal sickness, she stared, appalled at the skeleton that had once been her lover. Unconsciously she put her arm around the boy's shoulders and hugged him. Tom Fytton was growing tall and strong, but he was still a boy for all that. An impish grin and a mischievous nature and a mind of his own. Like his mother.

"You came." Geoffrey tried to smile, though the effort was almost too much. Then he saw that she held her younger son to her and he closed his eyes to shut out the pain. Why? Why even now did she find a way of hurting him? He turned his face to the wall.

"Geoffrey." Her voice was choked with emotion. "Look at him. Please."

He turned his head then and she saw

the old flash of hatred in the black, brooding eyes. "A fool to the end," he managed, in a cracked and bitter voice.

"Leave us, Tom. There's a good lad." She pushed him towards the door. He was only too willing to be out of the foul atmosphere and lost no time in finding Belle.

Isabel wiped the archer's brow. He was burning up. "Geoffrey. Can you hear me? Can you understand?" She took his wasted hand in hers. "He is yours. Tom is your son. I swear it. That night, when I came to you here . . . the night Adam Banaster died . . . it was for a purpose. Thomas would have murdered you too, had he known our plans. I had to make you hate me. For your sake. For Christiana's sake."

He opened his eyes. "Liar! What have I done to deserve such torment . . . "

"Oh, Geoffrey, my love. Can you not see? They would never have allowed it. It would have been the Gallows Field. You know it would. And how could I have lived then? Knowing I had killed you? And that wonderful night, when we loved until we could love no more, our second son was conceived. On the love of the Virgin, I swear it!"

He wanted to believe. Desperately. Could it possibly be true? Tom was his son? And Isabel had loved only him in all her life? He saw the tears, hot and heavy, roll down her cheeks. He saw her mouth tremble with the thousand kisses she had saved for him alone. But after a lifetime of hoping and losing, how could he ever trust her?

"I believe her, Father." They hadn't realised that Jordon had entered. "I think I knew from the first time I set eyes on him, when he was no bigger than a flea. And, as I recall, he tried to sting me with his little wooden sword. There was something . . . I don't know what, but something that reminded me. And now I know. He reminded me of you. The fire. The temper. That anger deep inside. I suffer from it too, at times." He was prosperous. He was respected in London. But he could never forget his origins. Or his family.

Geoffrey Bernulf found new strength in his limbs and he lifted himself up to reach under the sacks on which he lay. Finding what he was looking for he held out his hand. "Take it," he ordered Jordon. Then he nodded his head, a smile on his ravaged face as he looked at the woman he loved. "If only! My life has been lived by that worthless motto. I had more than I deserved, had I but known it. The true love of two good women. And if I hadn't been so selfish I might have seen it and been happy."

Jordon had been studying the object in his hand, turning it over and over. "Is it . . . ? It can't be a ruby! Not one so large!"

"Gaveston's ruby," Geoffrey almost choked on phlegm as he tried to laugh. "It has been in my possession for many years."

The scene before his pain-filled eyes receded until only the stink of death remained. Before him, clear and sharp, was the handsome face of Piers Gaveston, bosom friend and intimate companion of the King. Even closeted inside the dismal cell within the walls of Warwick, caught in a dangerous web of his own making, he somehow exuded confidence and charm. Geoffrey marvelled again at the bright, intelligent eyes; the strong square chin; the full, still smiling mouth. As he had held out the flashing ruby to the overawed archer, had he known it was already too late? Had he known that the axe was destined to sever his neck before the sun set in the evening? Had he smelt death on his swarthy skin as Geoffrey Bernulf struggled with its vile odour in his nostrils today? The glittering fire of the gem had blinded the peasant to the courtier's predicament. He had scarcely given it a thought. But the ruby! That precious stone! It had been the key to his heart's desire.

"Ah. Such foolish dreams." The ghost from the past faded and he was again surrounded by the shadowy figures of the present.

"Father?" Jordon knelt at the dying man's side and touched the parchment-dry skin of his withered hand.

"Take it ... " Geoffrey tried to swallow but his throat was tight and aching. "Once ... " He sank back gasping. From somewhere deep inside he summoned strength. "Once, I thought it would buy me all the love I had ever wanted . . . " His dimming eyes sought out Isabel in the gloom. "But love cannot be bought. If it isn't given freely, then it is worthless . . . "

"Geoffrey . . . " Isabel bent towards him.

"You know it is the truth." He managed a tired smile. "And for all the good it has done me, I might as well have used it to buy the services of a whore when I was young. But perhaps God has his reasons after all . . . " he feebly squeezed Jordon's hand. "It is on my conscience that the young King still searches for those who murdered his father, never thinking his parent could be safely across the sea. Go to him. Tell him the truth . . . "

"With Mortimer and the Queen ruling . . . ?" Jordon was incredulous.

"Gaveston's ruby will gain you secret entrance to the boy. And give credence to the tale." Geoffrey's grip on his son tightened. "The relief that his mother's soul is not perjured will bring you a reward." The archer's misty eyes burned briefly with the old determination. "Remind him of a certain prisoner, still mouldering within the Tower . . ."

Isabel gasped.

" . . . and ask for the release of Thomas Fytton." He saw tears glisten on Isabel's cheek and his voice wavered with emotion. "I cannot leave you defenceless . . ."

Jordon de Bolyn rose from the side of his father's death-bed and, taking his mother's hand, raised it to his lips. "My father is wise. You are strong, but still you are only a woman. And a woman needs a man." He smiled slowly as an idea came to him. "And for my part, I return that which is truly yours. Gawsworth Hall. To be given, in the fullness of time, to my brother. Your other son." His words encompassed both his parents. "My own future lies in London, where I shall endeavour to found a second dynasty."

Geoffrey lay back, exhausted but knowing he would die contented. The bloodline would continue. A Bernulf would be master of Gawsworth. And another would manipulate the Port of London.

Outside the cottage, October's sun

was cool and Christiana shivered as she watched the children, heads together, examining a stone. Or a leaf. Or a dying insect. The rich chestnut of the de Orrebys contrasted strongly with the bright, fiery tangerine of the Banasters. Both different again from the gloss-black hair of the man now emerging from the fume-filled interior of the tiny dwelling. Jordon de Bolyn was the living image of Geoffrey Bernulf and the witch-woman thought, not for the first time, how strange life could be. Isabel had borne him two sons. And yet it was Belle, the bastard daughter of a murderer, who had been the joy of his last years. Belle. The child they had never had. The child who had been their family. Made them complete.

She started as Isabel touched her arm and the two women, rivals for so long, stood close. United in grief. Tears, quelled for his sake, spilled out unchecked as they faced together an event neither had ever imagined. They cried for him. For his pain and suffering. For the boy he once was. For the man he became. For the heart-rending, heaven-sent love they had shared.

From the darkness, he called. The tall, slim woman in velvets and furs turned away. Christiana was the name on his lips. Only she could give the relief he craved. And she would be the one to cradle him to her breast as he breathed his last. There was nothing Isabel of Gawsworth could do to alter that.

* * *

All Hallows Eve. Three Mile Wood wore russet and gold, not knowing. He was dead. Isabel sat amidst autumn's glory, thinking. Yet not able to think. He didn't breathe this air. Feel this sun. The world was suddenly empty of everything she had ever known. Their lives had been separate, yet so entwined that she had never thought that one day she would awaken to find herself alone. It frightened her and as darkness fell and she watched the sympathetic face of the silver moon waver through the almost naked branches of the forest she knew she didn't ever want to go home. She wanted to join him. In death.

Last night Jordon's messenger had arrived with the news that Thomas Fytton was released from the Tower on the orders of King Edward III, and that he was hard on the heels of the courier. He would be waiting for her now. Wondering where she was. Wondering why she was not there to greet him after six years of enforced separation. Wondering . . .

First frost glittered on branch and twig and moonlight scattered diamonds on the forest floor. Geoffrey had brought him home. Geoffrey, who had understood the loneliness his passing would leave, and as she had once given him into the hands of Christiana Marton, so he gave her into the safe-keeping of Thomas Fytton. Slowly she rose from her green-cushioned couch and stretched the stiffness from her limbs, and with her heart and mind empty of all hope she made her way back to Gawsworth Hall.

★ ★ ★

He had not bothered to light the torches in the bedchamber, but stood, gazing out over the black and silver landscape, not even turning as she entered.

"I never noticed it before." His voice was gruff, struggling with unaccustomed emotion. "The space. The depth. The beauty. It deserves the finest Hall in Cheshire, and by God I shall build it." He half turned, almost embarrassed to look at her. His wife. "There was much I didn't notice."

Isabel twisted the silken tassel on her girdle round her fingers nervously. She closed her eyes and prayed. "Dear God, help me." The words were silent. Screaming inside her head.

"There was much I took for granted." His voice had softened. When Isabel opened her eyes, he hadn't moved. Not made a single step towards her.

"I have seen the things you have achieved whilst . . . whilst I have been away. The estate is richer by far than when I left." His words became husky. "And I have seen my son. You are more than I deserve . . . "

Isabel felt numb. The blood drained

from her face and she felt that she would faint. This was not the man she remembered. This was not the man whose only thoughts were rape and murder.

"He is a fine boy . . . " There was a catch in his throat and the glisten of a tear in his eye. "Isabel. Forgive me."

Forgive him? Isabel felt a sudden rush of shame and guilt. What had she done? How could she have known? His son was not his son, nor ever could be.

"Please . . . "

She could feel the tension as he waited, not knowing what to expect. She could see his strong profile against the moonlight, and sense the masculine vitality imprisonment had failed to quell. He was more than the brutal soldier she had thought him. He was a man. A man who had had time to reflect on life and had found himself wanting. Which was ironic. She was no saint, either.

Isabel moved slowly towards him, her heart pounding. She stood before him. Placed her hands in his. And lifted her face.

Carefully. Cautiously. His mouth sought hers, tasting her acceptance. Then, with tears forcing their way from under her tightly closed lids, she put her arms around his neck and clung to him. They had been given a second chance. And God willing, she would one day present him with a child.

THE END

***Other titles in the
Ulverscroft Large Print Series:***

TO FIGHT THE WILD
Rod Ansell and Rachel Percy

Lost in uncharted Australian bush, Rod Ansell survived by hunting and trapping wild animals, improvising shelter and using all the bushman's skills he knew.

COROMANDEL
Pat Barr

India in the 1830s is a hot, uncomfortable place, where the East India Company still rules. Amelia and her new husband find themselves caught up in the animosities which seethe between the old order and the new.

THE SMALL PARTY
Lillian Beckwith

A frightening journey to safety begins for Ruth and her small party as their island is caught up in the dangers of armed insurrection.

THE WILDERNESS WALK
Sheila Bishop

Stifling unpleasant memories of a misbegotten romance in Cleave with Lord Francis Aubrey, Lavinia goes on holiday there with her sister. The two women are thrust into a romantic intrigue involving none other than Lord Francis.

THE RELUCTANT GUEST
Rosalind Brett

Ann Calvert went to spend a month on a South African farm with Theo Borland and his sister. They both proved to be different from her first idea of them, and there was Storr Peterson — the most disturbing man she had ever met.

ONE ENCHANTED SUMMER
Anne Tedlock Brooks

A tale of mystery and romance and a girl who found both during one enchanted summer.

CLOUD OVER MALVERTON
Nancy Buckingham

Dulcie soon realises that something is seriously wrong at Malverton, and when violence strikes she is horrified to find herself under suspicion of murder.

AFTER THOUGHTS
Max Bygraves

The Cockney entertainer tells stories of his East End childhood, of his RAF days, and his post-war showbusiness successes and friendships with fellow comedians.

MOONLIGHT AND MARCH ROSES
D. Y. Cameron

Lynn's search to trace a missing girl takes her to Spain, where she meets Clive Hendon. While untangling the situation, she untangles her emotions and decides on her own future.

NURSE ALICE IN LOVE
Theresa Charles

Accepting the post of nurse to little Fernie Sherrod, Alice Everton could not guess at the romance, suspense and danger which lay ahead at the Sherrod's isolated estate.

POIROT INVESTIGATES
Agatha Christie

Two things bind these eleven stories together — the brilliance and uncanny skill of the diminutive Belgian detective, and the stupidity of his Watson-like partner, Captain Hastings.

LET LOOSE THE TIGERS
Josephine Cox

Queenie promised to find the long-lost son of the frail, elderly murderess, Hannah Jason. But her enquiries threatened to unlock the cage where crucial secrets had long been held captive.

THE TWILIGHT MAN
Frank Gruber

Jim Rand lives alone in the California desert awaiting death. Into his hermit existence comes a teenage girl who blows both his past and his brief future wide open.

DOG IN THE DARK
Gerald Hammond

Jim Cunningham breeds and trains gun dogs, and his antagonism towards the devotees of show spaniels earns him many enemies. So when one of them is found murdered, the police are on his doorstep within hours.

THE RED KNIGHT
Geoffrey Moxon

When he finds himself a pawn on the chessboard of international espionage with his family in constant danger, Guy Trent becomes embroiled in moves and countermoves which may mean life or death for Western scientists.

TIGER TIGER
Frank Ryan

A young man involved in drugs is found murdered. This is the first event which will draw Detective Inspector Sandy Woodings into a whirlpool of murder and deceit.

CAROLINE MINUSCULE
Andrew Taylor

Caroline Minuscule, a medieval script, is the first clue to the whereabouts of a cache of diamonds. The search becomes a deadly kind of fairy story in which several murders have an other-worldly quality.

LONG CHAIN OF DEATH
Sarah Wolf

During the Second World War four American teenagers from the same town join the Army together. Forty-two years later, the son of one of the soldiers realises that someone is systematically wiping out the families of the four men.

THE LISTERDALE MYSTERY
Agatha Christie

Twelve short stories ranging from the light-hearted to the macabre, diverse mysteries ingeniously and plausibly contrived and convincingly unravelled.

TO BE LOVED
Lynne Collins

Andrew married the woman he had always loved despite the knowledge that Sarah married him for reasons of her own. So much heartache could have been avoided if only he had known how vital it was to be loved.

ACCUSED NURSE
Jane Converse

Paula found herself accused of a crime which could cost her her job, her nurse's reputation, and even the man she loved, unless the truth came to light.

BUTTERFLY MONTANE
Dorothy Cork

Parma had come to New Guinea to marry Alec Rivers, but she found him completely disinterested and that overbearing Pierce Adams getting entirely the wrong idea about her.

HONOURABLE FRIENDS
Janet Daley

Priscilla Burford is happily married when she meets Junior Environment Minister Alistair Thurston. Inevitably, sexual obsession and political necessity collide.

WANDERING MINSTRELS
Mary Delorme

Stella Wade's career as a concert pianist might have been ruined by the rudeness of a famous conductor, so it seemed to her agent and benefactor. Even Sir Nicholas fails to see the possibilities when John Tallis falls deeply in love with Stella.